MW00344018

DESTINYQUEST

Also by Michael J. Ward in the DestinyQuest series

The Legion of Shadow

The Heart of Fire

The Eye of Winter's Fury

The Raiders of Dune Sea

Visit the official website at: www.destiny-quest.com

DESTINYQUEST
The World Companion

Michael J Ward
Illustration by David Wyatt

Matador
Unit E2 Airfield Business Park,
Harrison Road, Market Harborough,
Leicestershire. LE16 7UL
Tel: 0116 2792299
Email: books@troubador.co.uk
Web: www.troubador.co.uk/matador
Twitter: @matadorbooks

ISBN 978 1803134 819

British Library Cataloguing in Publication Data.
A catalogue record for this book is available from the British Library.

Typeset in 12pt Calibri by Troubador Publishing Ltd, Leicester, UK

Matador is an imprint of Troubador Publishing Ltd

For Mary
Who has been with me from the start.
Who has been at my side through every high and low.
This is a celebration and a thank you for your faith in me.

Foreword

When I first started writing DestinyQuest over ten years ago, I was setting out to create a specific gaming and reading experience, one that would capture my enjoyment of action RPGs, such as *World of Warcraft* and *Diablo*. That enjoyment, I will freely admit, came more from the looting and levelling, and less so the storytelling.

When it came to writing *The Legion of Shadow*, I somewhat followed that model, with the emphasis skewed more towards the fun game stuff like character customisation, combat and looting, rather than the story. That was what got me excited – and I hoped that readers would agree with me. The story was really only a tool to move the hero from one theatre of war to the next, to stack up opponents and allow readers to let loose with their abilities (and dice!).

However, as I started to plan the second instalment, *The Heart of Fire*, the feedback from the first book was, quite rightly, mixed – with some people loving the book for its combat system and challenge, whilst others found the choices and worldbuilding somewhat lacking. I took this feedback onboard and set out to make *The Heart of Fire* the best gamebook I could possibly write.

By this stage, I felt comfortable with the game system, so that gave me more freedom to focus on the story and its choices – giving players greater agency in the world to make meaningful decisions. *The Heart of Fire* really marked a pivotal moment in my gamebook writing, where I felt that I could provide something really unique and immersive. And so, that's when I started to take lore more seriously, making copious amounts of notes about the Kingdom of Valeron and the world as a whole – its magic system, the various towns and cities, their history, key characters, world-changing events and so on. And this has continued throughout the series, leaving me with a huge stack of notepads filled with scribbles, maps, timelines and character sketches.

What I've always found tricky with gamebook writing is getting those kinds of details into the narrative. I know the DestinyQuest books are big, but believe it or not, I am often wrestling for space and a lot of stuff gets cut out. It can be frustrating at times, because there are occasions when I want to 'open up' more of the world and its lore to the reader, but I also have to consider page count and keeping the main action/narrative flowing. While I have certainly planted many nuggets amongst the books that allude to the larger world and its backstory, I've never really had the chance to share all those details with fans.

Until now.

The material in this book was originally written to accompany a roleplaying game product based on the DestinyQuest series. While that project sadly didn't make it to fruition, it did leave me with a ton of source material that I knew fans would love to delve into. So, rather than let all that material go to waste, I decided to publish it as *The World Companion* – which is the book that you now have in your hands.

At last, I can share with you some of the rich lore of my world – stuff that I literally have never been able to cram into my gamebooks, but can now finally release into the wilds. Hopefully, it will provide you with an exciting glimpse into the war-torn Kingdom of Valeron and the conflicts (and characters) that have shaped its history – and may yet play a part in its future.

I really hope you enjoy taking this journey with me across the world of DestinyQuest. Strap on your backpack and grab that sword – it's time to go adventuring!

Michael Ward

Michael J. Ward

Contents

1
The Creation

In the beginning, there was only Yu'Weh – alone and adrift in the endless void. His dreams were of emptiness, his eyes closed and unseeing. Then a spark ignited a dream of life. For he was but one in the nothingness, a singular light in the sea of darkness. In his mind he pictured another. And from his vast, fathomless mind, sprang Gabriel.

Made in his image, Gabriel was given the seed of destiny. His eyes were opened to stare into the void – and where his gaze fell, the stars spread across the blackness, a million shining jewels, their own light mirroring his own. A vast tapestry, illuminated by his exultant love.

Yu'Weh saw in his mind's eye the beauty his son had created. And was pleased. Such beauty stirred his dream in a new direction, to a fresh purpose. A plan. A vast cosmic design that would spill life throughout the darkness, forever filling it with that same eternal joy. He took that thought – that unflawed vision of beauty – and crafted a woman. A companion for his son. He named her Kismet. And the delight of creation would forever be her gift.

Kismet desired life. And Gabriel saw her purpose. Together, their union birthed a third. They named her Aisa. She was to bring balance – for where there was life, there now had to be death. Her sweeping gaze ended stars, turning light to darkness, existence back to emptiness.

A Grand Plan

These were the three Fates. Created at the very beginning of time. Yu'Weh stirred in his slumber once more, his dream exposing more of the great plan – the pieces now tumbling together, their picture forming with a greater clarity. This was to be a celestial scheme of grand ambition, one that might even wake him from the eternal sleep. His thoughts brushed against the three Fates, instilling within their souls their purpose in the plan.

Each Fate was granted three worlds – three spheres of life – that would embody the very essences of their elemental strengths. Nine worlds in total, each moulded by the will of its creator, and placed in an assigned space within the vast void.

The Nine Worlds
Each celestial Fate created three worlds,
dominated by a main element:
 Gabriel – Cahdia (light), Kayu (wood), Logum (metal)
 Kismet – Terra (earth), Dormus (fire), Vodena (water)
 Aisa – Umbril (shadow), Shadhaka (lightning), Anach (air)

Again, Yu'Weh stirred, his mind impressing itself upon his three celestial servants, granting each their power and position within the plan – to see it through to its ambitious finale. Kismet was the spinner and from her, life blossomed in silken strands of radiance. A vast and tangled webwork of individual lives, spilling light back into the void. This bright tapestry would fill the nine worlds with the elder races – dwarves, elves, kreen and fey – who would be their caretakers; guardians that would tame and master each element, turning worlds to vibrant paradises.

Gabriel was the weaver, the master of destiny. Within each life, each thread, he saw their individual journeys, their interactions, their hopes and dreams – a dizzying myriad of choices. He took the silken strands, birthed from his beloved, and fashioned the disparate parts into a cohesive whole, an intricate weave that would see the plan through to fruition.

Aisa was the ender – the cutter of the web. Because now, as before, there also had to be death. Each final heartbeat, every last breath, those were her music, the dark symphony that sang in her heart. When they called, her scythe would reap those lives, cutting away the strands from the weave – their light flickering and winking out to darkness.

But with each ending, the energy of that death would spill back to its source and Kismet would spin once more, turning death to life. And so, the cycle was in motion – forever spinning, the power of its vibrant force showering the darkness once again with stars, burning bright and then dying to embers – then flaring once more into brilliant being. Death and life in an endless dance, a perfect union.

Then came rebellion...

Battle of the Fates

Aisa grew impatient with the plan. Watching these small lives glittering before her, they became an irritant, a reminder of the ignorance of these mortal creations. They were foolish and blind, and slow to action. Gabriel was giving them purpose and enlightenment to help guide their steps, but it was like pouring treasures into crude vessels. These mortal beings were incapable of any lasting achievement. Slowly, resentment turned to jealousy. How was it that these contemptable creatures could love and bring life to their worlds – to enjoy companionship, loyalty, desire, passion? Aisa implored the great Yu'Weh for a companion, so that she might finally have offspring of her own. But her pleas went unanswered. Yu'Weh ever slumbered and his mind was closed to her supplications.

Aisa's soul became inflamed with anger and rejection. Her gaze turned to the nine worlds, still so desperate in their infancy, their peoples struggling to tame their environments. The plan could take eons, an infinity of time – and to what end? She didn't truly grasp the outcome; such things were kept from her knowing. Only Yu'Weh and Gabriel knew the true design – a mystery held secret.

And so, Aisa rebelled. Her gift was to end lives, to cut threads. Now, she wanted to end entire worlds. Raising her cosmic scythe, she swept it across the void, its perfect edge slicing through the weave. Thousands of lives screamed out of existence, the symphony of death a deafening crescendo. Her rage was inconsolable. Aisa sought to destroy everything, to bring the plan to ruin and reduce the weave to a final silent darkness.

Gabriel and Kismet implored Yu'Weh for aid, but he was lost in his torpor, his mind made restless by tortuous nightmares. Worlds were falling to ruin as life energies spilled from the severed weave – lives ended before their time. Each one brought wracking pain to Gabriel and Kismet, for their own essences were invested in each and every life.

Aisa would not stop. Death of such magnitude was like a heady addiction. She was deaf to the angered entreaties of her fellow Fates. Rage had taken over and she had become consumed by it. Gabriel and Kismet had no choice but to go to war with their own offspring. The battle was fierce, a cosmic display of elemental energies. Their wounds bled across the vastness – and each injury, each interchange of blows, left the Fates forever changed.

In a last effort, Kismet used the powers invested within her – the burning energy gifted her through the millions of deaths that Aisa had wrought – and used them to craft a prison. Celestial chains were cast around Aisa, dragging her down into a limbo known as Hel, where her screams would no longer be heard.

The rebellion was ended. But worse was to come.

The Weave Undone

Gabriel was weakened from the fight. A critical wound was slowly bleeding away his essence, spilling stars into the void. Worse still, his newfound blindness impaired his ability to guide the weave. With no cutter to end lives at their preordained time, the weave was turning into a chaotic confusion that was proving impossible to set on course.

Kismet also suffered in the aftermath of that war for she had become corrupted with Aisa's essence. The lives she was spawning were now a myriad of forms. Some twisted and tainted, like goblins, dragons, trolls, giants... things that should never have seen the light of creation. And others too, that perhaps were doomed by their imperfections, but had something of that original light in their souls – humans. These new lives fed into the weave, crossing into the nine worlds. Gabriel tried to knit these imperfections back into some semblance of the original plan, but his blindness and weakness were not up to the task.

Yu'Weh trembled and convulsed – his mind still gripped in nightmares without end. His cosmic vibrations swept across the void, washing against Aisa's prison and weakening her bonds. Aisa broke free of her chains, her rage now something that had consumed her to madness. From a tortured heart of darkness, a force known as the Shroud spread forth. It was her own weave, her own dark plan – to engulf the worlds and destroy them. She had the power of creation now, for Kismet's essence was a part of her – a power stolen through their warring and strife.

The Shroud spread quickly like a malignant virus and within its swirling chaos, the demons sprang forth. They were born from Aisa, her own children at last – a manifestation of her tortured soul. They wielded powers borne from their volatile realm. This new weapon, known as magic, would prove unstoppable.

The Shroud pressed close to each world, tearing down the fabric of realities, until demons in their vast legions could spill forth into the physical realms, to pillage, dominate and destroy. Gradually, one world fell after another as its peoples were either enslaved or consumed entirely by the Shroud. And each lost world fed its primal energies back into that malignant maelstrom, birthing elemental spirits as dangerous as their demon-brethren.

Gabriel's Sacrifice

One world remained untouched. Gabriel could see no hope for the original plan, his own efforts to save it having proved futile again and again. Growing ever weaker, he knew the people of this ninth world – the world of Dormus – would not withstand the might of Aisa's demonic legions. So, he chose to sacrifice himself. He poured the last of his celestial energies into the weave, suffusing those remaining lives with his vital essence. Their destiny would now be their own to seek and embrace – a power that could still guide the plan if they were able to work together, to be in union to battle the chaos. As his form splintered into rays of dying light, he found his sight miraculously returned as the mind of Yu'Weh was briefly with him at last.

Gabriel was given hope in that moment. And his fingers brushed a single thread of the weave, passing that hope into the grand plan. This one thread would be a messiah – the messenger to bring the word of truth to the people. To warn them and instruct them of what was to come.

On the world of Dormus, a shower of comets streaked through the night sky – the last breath of Gabriel visible for all to see. And at that moment, a young man was seen walking across the waves of a moon-lit sea. That man was Judah and he had come to preach the word of Yu'Weh – the word of the One God. And his message was simple. Aisa was coming for this world and the people needed to be prepared.

Dormus – the Heart of Fire

Each of the nine worlds shared something of the nine primal elements, but each was dominated by one. Kismet fashioned three worlds, one of which was born from her fiery hunger for creation – and, at its birth, no land was so fierce in the hostility of its landscape. Volcanoes spat smoke and sulphur into overcast skies, where geysers of flame would perpetually illuminate the low hanging clouds. The land itself was riven with lava and pools of bubbling magma, its oceans broiling with heat. Of those elder races that were scattered across the face of this brutal realm, only the dwarves were able to adapt to its ways and survive. The surface temperatures were scorching, the air itself a choking miasma that rarely abated. Survival meant going underground and the dwarves embraced their innate talent for stone craft, digging deep to find the cooler caverns below – far away from the sweltering world above. They became a subterranean race, living off the small creatures and fungi that desperately clung to life in this underworld realm.

For a thousand years or more, the world raged and boiled, seemingly forever burning bright. But then the world changed, perhaps as Kismet herself calmed and controlled her powerful appetites. She channelled earth and water to Dormus, dousing flames and silencing its wrath. The volcanoes smoked as many became dormant. Waters cooled the scarred landscape and from the fertile minerals that had been spewed from the depths of the underworld, the first plants began to take hold and thrive. This gradual transformation went unnoticed by the dwarves, who had shut themselves away – a reclusive race that shunned the light, their vast stone cities a refuge and a prison.

In the unseen heavens, Aisa's betrayal had sparked a cosmic war with her fellow Fates. Soon, the dwarves would find their realm beset by others, crawling up from the darkest depths: swarms of murderous goblins, giant arachnids, blood-thirsting trolls. War was indeed coming to Dormus – and the Age of Strife was about to begin.

2
The Domain of Magic

Aisa's creation, the Shroud, is a turbulent chaos of elemental energies. Within its writhing depths, whole worlds have been consumed and broken, their fragments forming a mosaic of crumbling islands, floating continents of ruin, and even whole realms that obey their own physical laws. With its birth came the demons – the offspring of Aisa. At first, such creatures were little more than embodiments of wrath and torment, with no higher thought than to destroy. Through their intense raw anger, they could create a physical manifestation of such rage – and this was the first magic to come into being. A volatile energy – a corruption of the celestial gift that each Fate commanded. Unlike their gifts of creation, magic had seemingly one purpose. To extinguish all mortal life.

As the many worlds slowly became enslaved or destroyed, the elemental energies spilling back into the Shroud started to shape the demons themselves – giving them greater powers and sentience, and moulding them into ever more deadly agents to serve their mistress' schemes. These volatile elements were also taking on their own unnatural life, shaped by the magics of the Shroud into creatures of fire, shadow, lightning, earth, air – some little more than figments of energy, others gargantuan giants with powers that rivalled the greatest of demons. These were the elementals and their numbers were legion.

Such forces have been growing ever stronger and more numerous, however – by contrast – Aisa's own power is now on the wane, her energies spent fighting against the confines of her prison. Yes, she had been freed from the initial chains that bound her and some of her malignant will has been able to manifest itself beyond the limbo in which she was cast. However, despite every attempt, she has never been able to fully break free of Kismet's hold – the energy of all those lost souls still, in some way, binding her in thrall. Instead, over the ages, she has impressed her plans and schemes on her demonic legions, but now that connection is weakening. The great Yu'Weh is stirring once again, his unsettled vibrations rippling across the void. She senses that his awakening might be close at hand and she might be powerless to stop it. Instead, her gaze is fixed on the greatest of her demonic and elemental followers, hoping that these will have the guile and strength to destroy the last world that stubbornly holds out against them. Surely, if that world falls, then her freedom will be guaranteed – and true vengeance against her heavenly enemies can begin.

A Hierarchy of Hate

Even within chaos, there is an order – of sorts. As the demons' power and influence has grown, a hierarchy has developed, a pyramid founded on the principle of survival of the fittest. Those with the greater strength have risen to the higher echelons of demon society and are able to dominate and command their weaker brethren. Many of these have forged these reputations in battle and conquest, others through the devotion of their mortal agents, who perform rituals and sacrifices to channel their faith into power for their demon overlords.

The greatest of these overlords is Shimaza, the master of shadow. It was through his cunning and tenacity that the world of Umbril fell to his will. That world is now under his total dominion, the few surviving mortals that remain now branded with his name and sigils, binding them as slaves – but also granting them immense power to serve out his nefarious schemes. These agents, known as the shadowborn or the Neverin, act as spies, assassins and even generals within his mighty demonic army, referred to throughout the realms as the Legion of Shadow.

Other overlords include Lagash, a demon lord of fire, and Azariah, a trickster who spins lies and deceit with mind magics born from the element of air. Each has agents firmly planted on Dormus, both of mortal and demonic origin, and – whilst they may, at times share common goals – more often than not, their loyalty is only to themselves. Their constant bickering, scheming and betrayals serve only to impede Aisa's ultimate goal – to bring the world of Dormus to ruin.

The elementals of the Shroud have a similar hierarchy, with lesser elementals in thrall to the greater elementals, who in turn obey the will of their elemental lords. Some of these wield vast power, although their destructive tendencies and single-minded nature encumber their efforts to supersede the demons. Nevertheless, Aisa is becoming increasingly aware of their value – as they are more easily commanded and bent to her will, especially as her ever-weakening powers continue to hinder her efforts to collude with the demons.

The Norr – Where Worlds Collide

The Shroud presses in on the world of Dormus, threatening to engulf it entirely. Where they meet and interchange their energies, there is a realm known as the Norr. Some mortals are able to project their spirits into this strange shadow-world, to traverse and explore it as if it was a physical region. Once their eyes grow accustomed to the swirling fogs and eerie corpse-light, they are presented with a landscape of nightmarish ruins and ravaged nature, almost a vision of Dormus' future should it finally fall. This unsettling hellscape is home to many elementals and demons, who hunt through the wreckage and malignant decay for those souls foolish enough to venture here of their own accord.

It is a dangerous path to walk. Should a mortal's spirit die in the Norr, such trauma is enough for the physical body to perish – or at least for the traveller to suffer extreme mental damage on their return. Even worse, such a spirit could become trapped, then their mortal body may waste away to death long before the spirit can rejoin it. In such cases, that spirit will be forever damned, becoming an eternal prisoner of the Norr.

Whilst such dangers exist, some mortal mages and shamans of Dormus still choose to walk this place, sometimes to commune with elementals and demons. Many treasures and artefacts also find their way into the Norr, perhaps spilling from tears in the fabric of both the physical plane and the Shroud – powerful items that are imbued with potent magics. For those with the aptitude, these can be brought back into the physical realm. Nevertheless, even the most mighty of mages and shamans are wise to prepare diligently for such a journey and guard themselves thoroughly with protective wards, should the deadly forces that exist there choose to mark them out as prey.

Both a Master and a Slave
The elemental energies that persist within the Shroud (and its lesser realm, the Norr) are what mortals can shape into magic in the same manner as the demons. Where the borders between these realms are weak or torn entirely, then the Shroud's corruption can leak into the world. Those exposed to it may not even be aware of it, until the strange energies start to manifest themselves.

Magic primarily draws on emotion – usually anger and rage. Hence, for those infected by the Shroud, the first sign of their dormant powers is often revealed during moments of violence or extreme stress, and this can lead to catastrophic results for both the victim and those around them.

By its very nature, magic is volatile and difficult to master. Those that first discover their talent are known commonly as wild mages, for they have yet to gain a disciplined understanding of the forces that they wield. As such, they remain a constant danger – for such elements are destructive and powerful. Very few wild mages live long enough to gain control over their magic, for they simply cannot regulate these powers without doing damage to themselves. Burns, frostbite, and even necrosis, are common ailments that can expose a struggling wild mage to others.

However, mastery of the art is possible through study, practice and patience. For this reason alone, the University of Magic in Valeron and its outlying colleges, were set up to help mages gain such a knowledge within a controlled environment. Nevertheless, the existence of such establishments has always been divisive – with many holding to the belief that magic should be stamped out entirely, for the potential harm it can cause to others. The Church in particular, which exerts a firm hold over Valeron society, views magic as a demonic taint – and those that wield it are branded heretics that pose an insidious threat to society. The Church's influence has played a significant role in denying aid to many who have fallen foul of such a taint. Only the wealthy and well-connected, mostly from the noble families, gain the opportunity to further their skills in the sanctuary of the university and colleges. Those without such advantages are typically ostracised – and can become prey for the witchfinders and inquisitors, who have no qualms about ridding the world of such wild magics.

Unlocking True Power

Despite the dangers and challenges of the craft, some mages with the requisite intelligence and willpower are able to exert a modicum of mastery over their powers – eventually becoming either a bane or a boon to society, depending on their whims. However, magic is addictive and as such, many are continually driven by an insatiable thirst for power, desiring ever more potent abilities. Such mastery can only be achieved through a receptacle of power known as a kha.

Each and every demon or greater elemental is powered by a heart of energy known as its kha. If a mage can acquire such an item – usually by defeating a demon or elemental in combat – then they can start to attune themselves to the kha and absorb the powers trapped within it. At first, these can present an immense boon for an eager mage, elevating their magical strength to new and almost frightening levels of might. However, with greater power comes greater risks. Over time, the kha will exert its influence over the mage. Unless this connection is eventually severed, then the mage runs the risk of insanity or worse – becoming a living embodiment of the original demon or elemental they first defeated. Ending such a connection can be difficult. It takes extraordinary willpower and discipline, but if a mage is able to release themselves from such a bond, it is possible for them to maintain control of the powers they have learned. Such individuals, often referred to as archmages, represent the true echelon of magical expertise – becoming almost god-like as a result of the formidable powers they are now capable of wielding.

The Runework of the Titans

When Kismet became corrupted through her battle with Aisa, so the threads that she spun took on many imperfections. Some were so tainted that their strands were bereft of light, just filaments of darkness, almost invisible against the void. These imperfect creations magnified quickly over time, until the original strands of the weave – those elder races that had been raised up as part of the grand plan – were soon overwhelmed by a crisscrossing web of discordant chaos.

Below the heavens, the dwarves of Dormus were to experience the results first hand. From the tunnels and abyssal pits, the lesser creatures flooded forth – screeching and hollering for blood, seemingly driven by a bestial insanity that was beyond all reasoning. The dwarves were unprepared for such a bloodthirsty and unstoppable tide. Many cities fell under the first crashing waves before their populace even knew what was upon them. Those that did manage to muster some hasty defence – employing their picks, hammers and shovels as makeshift weapons – were still outmatched by the sheer number of foes. The dwarves fell back, abandoning whole cities to the goblins, trolls and other beasts of the dark – becoming vagabonds in their own caves and tunnels as they desperately sought sanctuary.

The dwarves needed something to even the odds. And they soon found it – in the titans that had come to Dormus. These celestial beings, also known as the Norns, had been guardians of the nine worlds, dreamt by Yu'Weh and given life into the weave by Kismet. As worlds fell to Aisa's vengeance and corruption, many of these titans lost their lives. Their threads were ended, but – as with all life – they were reborn again. And due to some quirk of their creation, the titans were able to recall their past lives and all the previous knowledge they had gained.

The weave spun them towards the world of Dormus, perhaps knowing that this world would eventually be key to the grand plan. They awoke deep within the underworld, formed of celestial light. They crafted new bodies for themselves out of the surrounding stone and earth, and marked themselves with sigils of power. When the beleaguered dwarves stumbled upon these strange beings, they feared they had discovered a new and deadly enemy. However, nothing could be further from the truth.

These titans were now blessed with a deep and profound understanding of the arcane – the very magic that had ended their previous lives. They could see into the Shroud and knew of the elementals that dwelt there and the powers these creatures could wield. Experience had also taught them that these elementals could be bound to the physical realm and made to serve a master.

The titans set about instructing the dwarves, revealing the symbols carved in delicate script across their immense stone bodies. These symbols, when drawn in a binding circle, could weaken the barrier to the Shroud and create a means of calling forth an elemental. Once made manifest, further runes carved into an object could then channel the elemental into that item, forcing it inside a confinement rune – where it would remain trapped and subservient. The dwarves set about hammering these runes into their picks and hammers, turning what was once regular iron into magical weapons, crackling with newfound powers.

And so, the dwarves began to reclaim their cities, a bitter struggle, but one that they were now capable of achieving. The lesser races certainly had numbers on their side, but tooth and claw were no match for the enchanted weapons of the dwarves. Outmatched, the goblins, trolls and other foul denizens were finally routed – forced to retreat back into the depths of the underworld or out onto the surface of Dormus, where the dwarves had no desire to follow.

The Lore of Language

The titans initially taught the dwarves the nine major runes, each related to their elemental force. These were then accompanied by eighty-one minor runes, which can interact and empower one another to create different enchantments, wards and effects. The dwarves went on to add to this complex language, developing further variations of these eighty-one runes. These became known as runic inflections and would slightly alter the nature of their primary rune and allow for greater flexibility in the way runes could be crafted together to spell out their patterns of power and magic.

The runes also led the dwarves to develop their own language of symbols to record their history and achievements. This became the first recorded language on Dormus. The dwarves would carve their script onto clay tablets using an iron stylus. Inevitably, many of these flimsy tablets were destroyed during the dwarven wars, but some vaults have been discovered intact, providing scholars with a treasure-trove of knowledge concerning the early history of Dormus. It is believed there may be more libraries buried or hidden deep in the ruins of the dwarven cities – waiting to be found by those with the skill and bravery to venture into such perilous depths.

Mastery of the Runes

Marking out and carving the runes was a difficult and dangerous task. Any slight imperfection in the work could lead to the elemental escaping its intended prison, leaving it free to wreak havoc in the physical realm. However, thanks to the careful tutelage of the titans, the dwarves gradually became masters of the art. Their many iron forges now rang with a new song, as armaments of war were crafted into being – axes, swords, breastplates, shields – all imbued with magic to withstand further trials. And there were many throughout the Age of Strife as the dwarven cities suffered constant harassment from goblin raids, troll warbands and beastly swarms. But each encounter, each victory and defeat, only strengthened their resolve – and pushed them to new heights of experimentation and learning, until their knowledge of runework surpassed even that of their titan teachers.

The dwarves would eventually pass from the face of Dormus, the crumbling ruins of their vast cities and fortresses a sombre warning of the fate that could befall any civilisation in troubled times. Nevertheless, their legacy has endured to this day, in the complex runelore now practised across Dormus – an art that was passed onto humans during the Dark Ages. Some might say that this artform is now at its zenith, perfected over a thousand or more years by the ingenuity and daring abandon of humanity – now evident in the dizzying patterns that can adorn weapons and armour, instilling a myriad of powers from their trapped elemental spirits.

Some runecrafters have pushed the art even further, forgoing some of the more elaborate summoning circles to scratch runes directly onto their intended target with the use of a magical stylus – itself runeworked in order to perform the summoning task. Only minor elementals can be summoned and bound in such a way, but it has enabled the art to become more accessible and widespread across Dormus. Nevertheless, because of the dangers involved, true artisan runecrafting remains a relatively rare profession, studied and practised only by those few with the discipline and acumen to master the complex language of sigils.

A Force of Nature

Dormus was the first world that Kismet conceived, hastily crafted out of a fervour for creation, but sorely lacking wisdom in its execution. Only the dwarves were truly able to endure the harsh conditions of a volcanic world – and only by digging deep into the earth and shunning the surface entirely. When Kismet's gaze finally returned to Dormus, she realised the error of her spirited ways and sought to rectify those mistakes.

Kismet focused her elemental powers, using the life-giving energies of water and earth to tame the unforgiving landscape – an effort to bring it closer to the verdant paradises that bloomed on Gabriel's worlds of Kayu and Cahdia. Her mighty earth energies coursed across the scorched continents, laying out a pattern of leylines, almost in imitation of the grand weave that spanned the heavens. Each leyline was a conduit for her energies, helping life to bloom from what had once been barren earth. Since their creation, these channels have continued to pulse with natural power, helping transform Dormus from a fiery desolation into a verdant life-sustaining world.

Return of the Fey

The fey were an elder race created by Gabriel. They thrived on the woodland world of Kayu, tending its lush forests and groves. They were a peaceful race, living in harmony with nature. Sadly, their paradise world was the first to be targeted by Aisa and her demonic forces. The fey were no match for the powers that were brought against them. Their forests burned, woodland cities destroyed, and the world – eventually – became consumed by the Shroud. However, their legacy lived on in the wood elementals that were now a part of the Shroud. These powerful beings did not share the same hate and destructive tendencies of their elemental brethren. Instead, they longed for life and to bloom once again – hence, the leylines of Dormus became an inescapable lure to them.

Where these leylines crossed, great conjunctions of natural power were created. The wood elementals were drawn out of the Norr to seek these life-giving energies. They manifested themselves as the first elder trees, planting their roots firmly into the leylines and drinking deep of their power. The presence of such spirits helped keep the leylines clean of the more virulent influences of the Shroud, ensuring that nature would continue to blossom across the face of Dormus.

As powerful spirit creatures, these mighty trees were capable of defending themselves, not only through powerful magic, but also in the colossal strength of their roots and boughs, which could animate and attack – strong enough to shatter the bones of a giant. However, as the lesser races continued to spread across the surface world, it became obvious the elder trees would need better protection.

These ancient spirits sought out guardians for their sacred groves. It was humans who answered the call. By drinking the enchanted sap of an elder tree, they were gifted with some of its power – a fusion of leyline energy and the magic of the Shroud. The females that took the sap became dryads, imbued with its natural forces. Despite their imperfect humanity, these lucky few were granted many of the gifts that had once belonged to the fey – from speaking with animals, to shaping wood to their will. The males, typically known as satyrs, were prone to more dramatic reactions to the sap. Their bodies would undergo violent transformations, bringing them closer in physicality to the original fey, but more likely to succumb to madness or worse as a result of their relentless metamorphosis.

The fundamentals of this nature magic were taught to other humans, namely the nomadic clans who often used the forests and woodland as a refuge from their enemies. These Wiccan tribes were not duty bound to protect the sacred groves, but often found themselves allied with the dryads in order to safeguard these precious havens from harm. This close bond between the two has continued to this day as the need for such woodland sanctuaries has become increasing vital in the violent end times.

Despite dwindling numbers, the Wiccan druids have continued the traditions of nature magic, passing it down from one generation to the next. Unlike the more volatile magics of the Shroud that invariably lead to insanity and death, the magic of nature – infused with the energy of the leylines – has proven easier to master and control, with less of the side-effects of its more destructive rival.

The Archons – a Vision of Hope

When Aisa turned against the other Fates, their battle was fierce and unrelenting. Each blow, each wound, led to an interchange of their energies. Just as Kismet soon discovered that her creative abilities had been tainted, so Aisa – once she had escaped the shackles of her initial imprisonment – eventually discovered that her demon offspring were not all fashioned by her own dark intents. Some aspect of Gabriel and Kismet were now an inescapable part of her, capable of miraculously fashioning law out of chaos. The first archons had been born – demons of light that were firmly opposed to the machinations of Aisa and her infernal legions.

Many of these light demons were unable to survive for long, as their numbers were few and the forces opposed against them innumerable. And yet, some did manage to carve out their own safe havens within the chaos of the Shroud – and from there, have sought to influence mortal lives in the physical realm ever since, in an effort to aid them against the other demons.

These powerful entities often appear as winged angelic beings – often haloed in dazzling white light. Whether this is their true form or one they choose to project is unknown. However, their sudden and unplanned existence may well have influenced Gabriel as he poured his life energies into the weave, and chose a mortal body to become a vessel for his final dying light. That mortal was Judah – and this man would change the world of Dormus forever.

3
Judah the Lightbringer

Valeron had risen to become the principal kingdom on Dormus, having conquered the lands of Amaral to the west and absorbed the shattered remnants of Franklin. These should have been times of rejoicing and optimism, but recent invasions had left Valeron weak and exposed. The lich of Perova had left much of the southern lands in ruin, the corpse-blight still clinging to those ravaged towns and villages – now considered lost and forsaken. To the east, the tribes of Mordland had finally united under a powerful leader and devasted the Kingdom of Franklin. Only luck had saved the Franks from complete annihilation. Although Mordland had retreated, riven with in-fighting amongst its khans after the death of their leader, the sheer destruction that had been wrought by their first invasion had been horrifying. To add further to the woes of such dark times, the Vaidskrig pirates had been successfully pillaging along the coast. Valeron had no navy to speak of and was poorly equipped to deal with such a threat. Thankfully, the Vaidskrig were only interested in loot and not settlement – and were finally routed when they sought to raid Valeron's capital city of Cairns.

Valeron had somehow defied the odds and still clung jealously to its hard-won lands, but the recent invasions had left a palpable air of fear in their wake. The royal coffers were almost run dry by the war effort and the taxes now levied on the people were harsh in already difficult times. Many towns saw rioting as a consequence – it was not a good time to be a royal tax collector. Burning effigies of the king was also becoming a popular pastime. Far from being the hero of the hour, he had become a figure of mockery and scorn. Now in his senior years and without an heir, there was uncertainty over the future succession. He had taken his third wife, a Frankish princess, who was barely on the threshold of womanhood. The royal wedding had been a lavish affair of feasting and celebration – for the nobles at least. Such blatant displays of showy extravagance only soured the populace further to their king and the elite. In some quarters there was talk of a people's rebellion, possibly stoked by the king's own brother, who jealousy coveted the throne.

Valeron was a kingdom that at any moment could implode, its glories set to the torch and its storied history trodden under the feet of angry mobs. In the towns and cities, there was muttering of a grand end, a final judgement that was coming. Pagan worship was rife, with bloody rituals and ceremonies giving honour to dark gods and nature spirits – a vain effort to find some token of hope and comfort in a world that now seemed bleak and uncertain.

Unbeknownst to this populace, seven individuals were making a very important journey. They had been called, having experienced the same vision. They did not know each other. Nor did they come from similar backgrounds. They simply found themselves drawn to a fishing town on the east coast of Valeron. Its name was Crowfoot. A bleak and unremarkable place, stubbornly clinging to the black rocks that gave the town its name. The people of Crowfoot had suffered more than most to the Vaidskrig raiding, having lost many to axe and blade, their homes reduced to charred ruins. A year or more had seen some progress towards normality, but they remained a community still broken by their experience.

On the night that the strangers arrived, a storm had been threatening to break all day, but now the clouds were clearing, moonlight washing over the Bay of Tears. Its waters were unusually still, the air itself charged with a strange and expectant energy. Overhead, cutting bright paths through the night sky, was a shower of white comets. An omen.

This night, a man would come to Valeron – his sandaled feet walking atop the waves of the bay. He was adorned in plain white robes, without mark or decoration, their paleness made bright by the glowing rod that he held aloft before him. This man was Judah. And he was bringing a message of hope to this beleaguered kingdom.

A Man for the People

Little is known of the man's youth, save the scant details provided in the scriptures. Judah was purported to be the son of a shipwright, raised in the coastal town of Morden, which would later be annexed by the sprawling city of Blackwater. His widowed father was his only family. At the age of seven, a sudden storm left both Judah and his father adrift in dangerous waters. Unable to right their course, their small vessel was smashed against a reef and both were lost to the churning waters. The corpse of the father was found several days later washed up on the shore, but not the young child. He remained missing and assumed dead – taken by the ocean.

Twenty-five years later, that child – now a man – was walking miraculously across the still waters of the bay to meet the seven strangers arrayed before him. The sight quickly brought others to the scene, mesmerised by the strange sight. According to the Book of Lucas, the first of the recorded scriptures, Judah spoke the following:

This is the time of fulfilment. Look for I am clad in righteousness and the light of the One God is in my heart. He has called you brothers and sisters to assist me. For we have much work to do. This land is sinful and the time for repentance is nigh. Do not kneel before me, as you would a king. I am your equal in all things – as every man, woman and child is equal in the eyes of the One God. He is light and love and judgement. So repent and walk with me and I will teach you the ways of the divine.

(Lucas 1: 5-6)

The seven strangers, who had been called by a shared vision, became Judah's apostles – those who would remain loyally at his side throughout his ministry. Others from the town also became disciples, drawn by the otherworldly nature of this man who purported to be a messenger of the One God.

And so, Judah and his followers began to tour the neighbouring towns. The scriptures record in detail how he healed the sick, the blind and the lame. He cast out the taint of the Shroud from those who had been caught by its lure, and he exposed the rituals and ceremonies of those who were venerating the demons and spirits. He wielded a power that he described as the 'divine light' and taught his followers how to call on that same power. The scriptures describe this as the inner kha – a core of holiness that, through the sacrifice of the One God's son, Gabriel, now resided in each and every life that was bound to the weave. Only with discipline, perseverance and prayer, could this inner kha be nurtured and encouraged to grow, so that its powers could manifest as divine miracles.

The power could also be used for wrathful judgement. When set upon by goblins, trolls and other monsters that roamed the wilds, Judah crafted his light into powerful bolts that could smite his foes. Word of such deeds quickly spread throughout Valeron – and soon, great crowds came to hear his teachings and see this blessed hero for themselves. At a time when the common people felt lost and downtrodden, his words gave them empowerment and hope. Whilst few, save the apostles, could tap into their kha and wield the divine light for themselves, Judah's miraculous displays were enough to win over hearts. But such growing popularity quickly drew the ire of those in power – the royals and the nobles, who feared where this loyal adoration might lead.

A Crown for a King

Outside the town of Castle Ford, later to be renamed Angel Ford in remembrance of Judah, there was a skirmish between soldiers and the followers of Judah. The soldiers had been sent to arrest him for treason. Judah intervened before blood was spilled, ordering his people to lay down their weapons. He surrendered himself to the soldiers, who manacled his arms and his legs, and took him by wagon to the capital of Cairns for an audience with the king.

What occurred is recorded in both the Book of Mary and the Gospel of Lamentations, authored by his youngest apostle, Timothy Sawyer. It is assumed Judah gave his account directly to these followers after his release.

Judah was marched through the streets to jeering crowds. The king had already been turning them against this man, branding him a trickster and a charlatan. In the royal throne room, he was brought before King Herald, who demanded to see the miracles of this One God for himself. But Judah refused. He was beaten and then whipped, and a crown of thorns set upon his head in mockery. The king called for a beheading, but as the blade was raised – Judah fixed his gaze upon the king and spoke:

'I know of the dream that torments you. None have been able to speak of its meaning. Not your sorcerers or soothsayers or worshippers of demons. I can tell you the meaning of your dream. My One God grants me that power. Will you listen?'

The elderly king visibly paled. And raised his hand to halt the execution. He then gestured for Judah to continue. And so, Judah interpreted the dream, recorded in the Book of Mary:

'Each night you see a dragon of golden scales, breathing fire over a vast sea. That dragon is Valeron and the fire is its might, for you will fight many wars in my name and for my God. The gold is your wealth, for I will show you the hills of gold and jewels that will bedeck your crown and give power to the dragon. You see the beast of shadow, a serpent, coiled around the dragon. It is caught in flame and consumed. That is Perova and you will conquer her lands. The final beasts are wolves, you hear them howling even now. The enemies at your door, those pagan peoples that bring ruin to all they touch. They howl and they scratch, but they will never harm the dragon. That which you must fear is the dragon of darkness, whose wings blot out the sky. Mordland will be a thorn in your side and you are both destined for strife until the end of days.'

(Mary, 7:15-18)

Silence befell the court, until the king finally responded. Despite being troubled by the accuracy of what Judah had described, he was still set on a bloody course. As the executioner's blade descended, white light blossomed from Judah – and the blade turned to ashes. To the shocked gasps of those present, Judah rose to his feet, his many wounds healing before their eyes. He addressed the king one more time:

> I know your wife is in pain. She lies abed and in the thrall of a deadly poison. Yes, it is not a fever that assaults her. She was poisoned by your brother. And the truth of my words will be found in his quarters. Take me to her and I will heal her. And I will put my hands upon her stomach, to bless the child she will carry. And you will name him after my father, Jotham.
>
> (Mary, 7:21)

Such revelations sent shockwaves throughout the court. True to Judah's word, the king's brother was found guilty and executed. The queen was healed and she would later give birth to a boy – who the king named Jotham. He would become a righteous king in his father's stead and would aid in the assembly of the first cathedrals. Judah also fulfilled prophecy by directing the king to the hills that he had spoken of on the outskirts of the city. These were later mined to reveal rich veins of gold, platinum and silver – turning around the fortunes of the city and of the kingdom. During the rule of later kings, the capital would be renamed Assay as a stamp of its newfound wealth and prominence.

The Anointed Angels
The king repented of his sin and released Judah, hailing him a hero of the kingdom – and granting free passage throughout Valeron. He also assigned his loyal knight, Davius Glint, as a personal protector for Judah. Reunited with his apostles and disciples, the expectation was that Judah would head west into the lands recently claimed from Amaral. Instead, Judah set his sights east, to the ravaged lands of the former Kingdom of Franklin.

The scriptures record many adventures on the perilous journey east, from the purging of haunted ruins to the founding of the holy city of

Antioch. During this journey, Judah showed his apostles how to inscribe holy script onto metal and into flesh. These lines of script, known as the sermons of light, would invoke divine blessings of protection and power. Glint's sword was the first to be marked in such a way. The apostles were also marked, the divine script branded into their skin – giving them greater command of their inner kha. He named these seven his anointed, angels that would carry on the work of the One God after his passing. Gifted with wings of celestial light, he directed them to spread the word across the world of Dormus. At first, they protested – not wanting to leave the side of their teacher and saviour, but Judah insisted it was part of the grand celestial plan. And so, at Antioch they bid farewell. They were never to see Judah again.

Death on a Mordland Cross

At sunrise, the morning after the anointed angels had left Antioch, the remaining disciples and followers of Judah awoke to find their leader gone. He had left in the company of Glint, and the two had headed out alone into the war-scarred wilds. This last journey is recorded in the final book of the scriptures, the Book of Ascension, penned by King Herald's royal chronicler, based on the account by Davius Glint.

Mordland had finally found itself a new king, Tenjin Khan. Unbeknown to Valeron, his forces were moving westward, looking to enact revenge for their previous inglorious defeat. The army was vast and fast-moving, and if it had gone unhindered, it would have likely devasted Valeron and changed history forever. But the One God had other plans.

Mordland outriders discovered Judah and Glint while they were scouting. Judah insisted that he have an audience with the khan to preach the news of the One God. He was led into the army encampment and granted his meeting. There, Judah delivered his great sermon recorded in the Book of Ascension. This sermon denounced the demons of the Shroud and called for an acceptance of the light. Mordland already had a long history of demon worship and many of their soldiers and priests wielded dark powers granted them through such practises. The khan mocked Judah's words, believing that the strength of his own demon patron, Asher, was stronger than any One God. And he would prove it, by murdering this god's foolish messenger.

Mordland had many bloody traditions, and one of these was crucifixion. Those captured in battle or had shamed themselves in service to their khan, could find themselves nailed to such a cross and left to die through suffocation or blood loss. Such a fate befell Judah. Glint was made to watch the grisly torture, knowing that he was to suffer a similar punishment the next evening.

Judah was still preaching, but his words went unheard, failing to carry over the jeering crowds gathered to feast and celebrate his death. That moment finally came as the sun was sinking in the west, casting a sanguine glow over the ravaged land. As he gave his last breath, a white light broke through the clouds, and fell across the gathered army. Within that light, they witnessed Judah ascend as a celestial angel – his mortal body cast away to ashes. From his back, wings of white brilliance spread wide, their pinions inscribed with holy script. The angel stretched out his arms and looked to the heavens. Then he spoke a single word, 'Yu'Weh'. There was a thunderous crack as a shockwave of force rushed out across the plain – and every Mordland soldier, including the Khan, was blasted to ashes.

The only survivor was Davius Glint, untouched by the wrath of the One God. When his sight returned following the blinding explosion, there was no sign of the angel – or the light from the heavens. Nor was there a single trace of the great Mordland army. According to historic records, over 46,000 Mordland troops died on that day – and cemented a blood feud between Mordland and Valeron, that would lead to countless wars across the ages.

Life After Death – the Endless Cycle

When the weave was created, there was an order to its arrangement of threads. Only Gabriel knew the ultimate plan of his father, the end goal of this marvellous creation. He instilled destiny into each thread, helping the millions of individual lives to further the plan. Each had a preordained moment of death, so that their failing energy could be cut off from the weave and fed back to Kismet, so that the energy could be restored and poured back into the weave. From death, there would be life again.

When Aisa rebelled and was imprisoned in Hel, there was no longer a cutter to end lives at their intended time. The plan was unravelling because chaos had now entered the weave – as well as the corrupted lives that Kismet was inadvertently spawning. Gabriel sacrificed his life to put the last of his power into the lives of the weave. For some, this energy shone brightly. These would be the ones to become great heroes and leaders of legend – the ones that could influence history and change the future. Others, may have shone less bright but still had their part to play.

When Judah came to Valeron, he helped his disciples to understand the work of the heavens. He described it as a process of reincarnation, where a life that was ended would be reborn again. If an individual had lived a good life and cultivated the divine light within themselves, then the new life would carry on that vital essence – that light – making it ever stronger. This was, in short, a key part of the plan: for the weave to grow brighter as good and moral lives flooded new threads with Gabriel's cosmic power.

Judah was speaking the truth. When a body dies, the soul rises and returns to Kismet to be reborn. In most cases, the new life will have no knowledge of the former. However, in some rare instances, the new thread may carry on some of the memory of its past life – so the individual might recall moments of a past that is not their own, or experience déjà vu as places and situations seem familiar. Rarer still are those that might even glimpse the future, due to the power of a past life giving them a greater insight into the vast interrelated threads of the weave.

Due to the ever-present influence of the Shroud, some souls do not have an easy route back to the creator, Kismet. The Norr can act as a barrier at times, where spirits might become trapped within the shadowy echoes of the real world. Often this might be through the influence of a demon or other entity, or simply as a result of the anguish of an agonising death or other deep-seated emotion that might tether a soul to the Norr – perhaps because of a task incomplete or a desire unrequited. These souls might then manifest as restless ghosts that can appear both within the Norr and also in the physical plane should they choose – trapped between worlds. Some may retain some intelligence and be able to interact in a limited way. Others may simply be nothing but pure emotion – be that sadness, anger, fear and so on.

These trapped souls can sometimes find a way to move on – or even, in rare cases, return to their former physical body if it hasn't decayed. It is believed many spirits, particularly the benevolent archons and wood elementals, have such powers to return a soul, but they are not freely given; there will always be a price to pay for a second chance at beating death.

4
The Church of Valeron

The news of Judah's death was a huge blow to the anointed and the other followers of the One God, but his willing sacrifice to save Valeron from Mordland's vengeance left a formidable and lasting legacy. The king declared an annual holy festival in Judah's honour – known as Ascension Day – and had a statue made of iron and gold erected at the centre of the capital. The Valeron calendar was also reset, with the year of Judah's ascension becoming year zero – and each year thereafter being referred to as year 'x' of the Ascension.

Judah was seen as a hero. After the dark days that had previously haunted the kingdom, there was a sudden air of optimism – as if Valeron had been specially chosen to receive such a blessing. From noble to commoner, the people were now open and ready to learn more about this extraordinary man and the faith that he had preached.

And so began the missionary tours of the seven angels. Blessed with the divine light, these imposing figures drew awe and devotion from all of those they met. The holy script, branded into their flesh, bestowed on them extraordinary powers – including a prolonged life. The last known angel to pass from the world was Timothy Sawyer at the age of 244, just one year prior to the outbreak of the fifty years war with Mordland that would eventually plunge Valeron once again into chaos and strife.

During their extended lifetimes, the anointed were instrumental in preaching the word, recording it in the scriptures, and providing aid to set up congregations in all the towns and cities of Valeron. Through inspired visions, the angel Erastus Dain drew up plans for ambitious building projects that would venerate the One God, from the imposing cathedrals that would channel sunlight into stunning displays of dazzling brilliance, to the churches that would soon become a common sight in every town and village.

Thanks to Gabriel's sacrifice, the lives of the weave were now blessed with his pure essence. That meant that every man, woman and child had the divine light inside of them. This power would vary from individual to individual. Some were blessed to discover this unaided, receiving visions from archons that would give them their calling. Others, despite all their efforts and devotion, would never truly connect with this power. Even for the pious, nurturing the kha and using it for miracles was an ability that was out of reach of most of the populace. It took the faithful years of dedication, devotion and persistent prayer, to be able to bring forth the light from the inner kha and craft it into healing energies, protective wards and fires of judgement. The angels sought to train as many as were willing, placing these within the congregations as leaders to inspire others. For the average commoner, even these individuals were looked upon with wonder and admiration, for few had the commitment to endure such long years of dutiful training.

Some of the anointed angels left Valeron in obeyance of Judah's instruction to bring the word of the One God to the world. Mary Malley travelled south. After setting up a successful congregation in the town of Stone Cross, she travelled onwards into the prairie lands and the jungles of the south – seeking out the reclusive tribes to teach them of the holy word. Timon Fray travelled east, helping with the efforts to rebuild what had once been the Kingdom of Franklin, before travelling across the ocean to Sargassi. Joseph Barnabas took the teachings to the desert lands of Khitesh, setting up a congregation in See-Val, the teeming capital of that affluent empire.

The anointed recorded everything they could during their missionary tours. These texts, whilst still considered the inspired writings of the One God, were later dismissed by the Church as non-canon to the main scriptures, and are now referred to as The Apocryphal Texts. Despite this, the writings contain many discoveries of new sermons of light that are still used in many of the church ceremonies and rituals today. Similarly, many of the anointed who travelled throughout the world of Dormus, erected shrines to mark stages of their physical and spiritual journey. These stone markers recorded their ongoing visions and sermons, granted them by their devotion to the One God. These would become highly sought after by pilgrims in later years, keen to record these for the Church.

The Sermons of Light
During his lifetime, Judah showed his seven apostles – who would later become the anointed angels – the art of inscribing holy script onto weapons, armour and into flesh. The delicate script was channelled from the inner kha, infusing each letter with the divine light. This procedure would draw deeply from the physical reserves of the individual. For Judah, this left no visible impression, for he was Gabriel's chosen one, and gifted with immense holy strength. Similarly, the anointed angels were able to perform the same rituals without serious consequences.

For those that they taught, who would carry on this tradition in the ages to come, the act would leave the caster physically drained. Persistent use of the art would often lead to premature aging, blindness, and eventually death. Only a rare few have proven to have the faith and desire to endure such training in order to perform these inscriptions, even when blind. Known as the white abbots, these holy individuals are often frail and ailing – no healing arts capable of restoring the life essence they lose each time they perform the rituals. Nevertheless, they choose to do so – to bless weapons and armour to ensure that the Church is able to exert its dominance over evil. And by inscribing such sermons in the flesh of the devoted, such as the holy inquisitors and paladins, they are able to elevate ordinary humans into powerful god-like beings, capable of unlocking new powers and abilities through their strengthened connection with the kha. This procedure is often referred to as anointing or baptising – and several abbots may lose their lives as a consequence of such a ritual. Hence, inquisitors and paladins are revered for the precious gifts they have been given at great human cost.

The First Crusade

During the time of the angels, Valeron enjoyed a golden age of reconstruction and expansion. New settlements sprang up in the recently claimed lands of Amaral and Franklin, and those areas that had been formerly corrupted by the plagues of Perova were cleansed by the angels' holy light. Devout pilgrims flocked eastward, to the holy city of Antioch – to witness the white rod of their saviour and the celestial fortress that it had summoned into being. Other former Frankish settlements were slowly restored and resettled. For a time, it seemed, Valeron was gearing up to become a world power of great renown. However, following the death of the last angel, that was all about to change.

Mordland had suffered greatly, but they were a hardy and tenacious people, forever willing to make great sacrifices for power and strength. A succession of wars had resulted in unification under a new and fierce leader, Altan Khutala. He had made dark pacts with many demons, and it was said that he was now more demon than man. Whilst magic in Valeron had been marginalised by the Church, in Mordland it was a celebrated practice. Their sorcerers had gained deep esoteric understandings of the arts through communion with their demon patrons. A brief alliance with the islanders of Vaidskrig had allowed Mordland to pillage the islands of Veda to the east. It was believed that Altan Khutala had discovered the famed Vedic texts that held secrets of the arcane – forbidden knowledge that surpassed even the runelore of the dwarves.

And so, with their strength renewed, Mordland looked to the west once again – to the lands where they had suffered shameful defeat. Each new generation had been taught of what had happened that fateful evening, when Judah ascended as an angel and brought holy wrath on the proud warriors of Mordland. That insult had gone unchecked – but now the time had come to exact revenge.

Many of Mordland's traditions had been swept away over the years to be replaced with an ever-increasing obsession with magic and demon worship. But one remained, and that was their skilled horsemanship. Their fast and mobile army could strike hard at their enemies. With the added might of their dark magics and runed arrows, they could unleash devasting and explosive assaults. Summoned elementals, in thrall to their sorcerer overlords, could blast defences with fire and ice, and unleash curses that left opponents blind and confused.

New Valeron was the first to fall – and then the towns and settlements scattered across the valleys and dales. The garrisoned knights and warriors put up a stalwart defence, but none were a match for the numbers arrayed against them. Unrelenting in their savagery, the Mordlanders put their enemies to the sword, razing buildings to the ground, and erecting grisly totems to mark each and every one of their victories. When they fell on Antioch, the city had been able to reinforce its defences with knights from Lull, but they did not prevail. A bitter siege, lasting several months, finally ended with the holy city falling. By now, news had reached the capital – and a crusade was launched to take back the lands of Judah. The current king, Metrias, implored the Church to bring its full force to bear. In Assay, the Order of Davius had recently been founded – a sect of holy knights with weapons and armaments blessed with sermons of light. It was hoped that these formidable warriors could stand up to the dark magics of Mordland and turn the tide of battle. They rode forth, becoming the first crusaders to formerly represent the Church in war.

Outside the city of Lull several great battles took place, with neither side gaining victory. A further series of advances and then retreats saw huge losses on both sides. Eventually, after years of gruelling hardship, Valeron was able to push Mordland back to Antioch, and retook the holy city.

The wars lasted half a decade, with frequent respites for rebuilding and consolidation punctuated with violent and bloody battles. Mordland was like an angry hound, continually beaten back but forever snapping at Valeron's heels. Antioch would change hands twice more in the campaign, eventually leaving the city little more than a devastated ruin – the celestial fortress created by Judah, the only structure untouched by the ravages of time and war. What had started as spirited optimism on both sides was soon lost to a long and bitter grind, sustained by pride more than any other real desire. Altan Khutala was not willing to give up, despite the losses and the suffering of his troops. Some say he had gone mad and was beyond all reasoning. He would not end his campaign until he was marching on the capital. And he almost got his wish, finally pushing through border forces in the Tallow Mountains to advance into the Sodden Hills. Raiding parties razed many towns and villages. Fear gripped Valeron, for no army had reached so deeply into its interior since the early days of Frankish incursions. But the marshy landscape did more to cripple the Mordland advance than any standing army. Their cavalry had lost their advantage, slowed by the water-logged fens and swirling fogbanks.

In the end, one of the generals mutinied and murdered the Mordland leader. His name was Arctus Jobiah. He had no desire for power, only to put an end to Altan's madness. After fifty years of hardship with no real gain, the Mordlanders were more than ready to go home to their lives and families. Valeron, likewise, was eager to put an end to hostilities. The Valeron general, Mallum Holt, met with Arctus Jobiah in the ruined marsh town of Black Slough and signed a treaty on behalf of their nations – pledging a hundred years of peace between Valeron and Mordland.

The War of the Princes
Peace can often bring more strife than good. A terrible crop-blight was spreading in the west, crippling food supplies. Disease was becoming rife and a spell of goblin raids against towns weakened by famine, saw Valeron once again suffering from misfortune. Wild magic was on the rise, probably due to the renewed interest in demons and pagan gods, with secret rituals becoming commonplace amongst the populace. Many blamed the One God for their hardships, having seen no gain and only punishment for their efforts during wartime. King Metrias was now in his eighties and his only heir had passed to a wasting disease. He became a paranoid recluse, fearing his rivals who coveted his power, and eventually the people as a whole – that seemed to be turning away from true worship with an air of possible rebellion. One of his final actions before his death, was to set up the inquisition. An order of holy warriors who, through force and intimidation, would impose the authority of the Church across Valeron. These formidable warriors

quickly became feared for their zealous belligerence in rooting out sin and rebellion. Rather than rallying a nation, their actions only served to sour an already frayed relationship between the commoners and the Church.

When the king finally died (of natural causes, so it was claimed), the country was plunged into turmoil as no clear heir had been decided upon. From such chaos, several contenders with dubious entitlements rose up to push their claims. One was a former Andal noble, another a distant cousin of the king's bloodline. Several battles ensued, dragging in other contenders as the state of the nation descended into a civil war that no one truly wanted or had a vested interest in. Finally, another candidate entered the fray – this one, having the backing of the Church.

This challenger was Hemides, a bishop and former war hero. With the power of the inquisition on his side, he was able to secure a swift victory and take the throne. He publicly declared that the One God had chosen him to set Valeron back on course. After the chaos and uncertainty, none were left to dispute this claim – and the commonfolk were just grateful to have some solid leadership at last.

The Witch Hunts
If they had known what was coming, the people of Valeron may have been less appreciative of their change in fortune. Throughout his reign, Hemides proved himself a religious extremist, determined to bring his own form of evangelist dogma to the Church. Taking Judah's last sermon as the crux of his edicts, he pushed for a doctrine of religious intolerance against those practising improper worship or worse – using magic openly, and putting others at risk. At this time, magic and some of the old ways were creeping back: it would seem a land ravaged by war and strife brought the influence of the Shroud pressing ever closer, with rips in the veil of reality letting foul creatures and their taint into the world.

The inquisition could only do so much to patrol the lands and provide protection and justice to the populace. So, Hemides commissioned a new order – of men and women who shared his zeal for stamping out sin and evil in all its guises. A renowned hunter of the period, known as Jasper Crane, played a significant role in what was to become the official order of witchfinders. He had already garnered a fearsome reputation as a hunter – having being born in Perova, a land still cursed by its tragic history. He had built up quite the knowledge of how its creatures could be dispatched, whether it was a stake to a vampire's heart, silver against a shapechanger or the use of blessed water to expose a witch or warlock. Hemides was fascinated by such artistry and commissioned Crane to set up a school, to train those of faith to become a force of evil-destroying professionals. This mysterious school, set within the city of Greyspire, was named the Acorlidge.

The Path of the Witchfinder

Most initiates to the school of the Acorlidge have usually already been acolytes of the One God for many years and/or have proved themselves on the frontlines of a battle or crusade. Over two years of study, a prospective student learns the gruelling arts and lore of the dark arcane, to better understand its insidious influences on society. After those two years, a graduate is classed as an apprentice and will shadow an experienced witchfinder until their master feels ready to grant them the title of witchfinder. This may take many years, depending on the bond and relationship of the two individuals. It is not unknown in more modern times for a witchfinder to pass his skills onto a stranger that he or she deems worthy of such gifts. If they see a willingness in their student to follow the One God and seek out evil, then they may share some rudimentary skills rarely disclosed beyond the secretive walls of the Acorlidge.

These grim-set rogues took on the mantle of their teacher, copying the characteristic long coat and broad-brimmed hat of Jasper Crane – which would quickly become a chilling identifier of these skilled hunters. They set about their work with a zealous abandon, looking to purge evil from the lands. The presence of a witchfinder would soon become a double-edged sword. Whilst being a source of comfort and protection in times of woe, they were also without mercy in their resolve. Anyone found to be suspicious of wild magic or worse, would suffer a death by burning – often with little in the way of a trial. These so-called witch hunts became common throughout the period of Hemides' reign and beyond, making the Church an institution to be feared as much as it was revered.

Hemides also moved the royal household to the newly named settlement of Solace, where the construction of a grand cathedral complex was underway, later known as the White Abbey. This grand venture would expand into a vast city and become a hub of pious learning and enlightenment for over a thousand years.

Hemides' son, Bevan, continued what his father had started, giving more power and influence to the Church in regards matters of the kingdom – and also created figureheads to represent such authority. These were Lord and Lady Justice, and were nominated for their positions by the bishops of the churches. They would hold their position until death and were considered the embodiment of Judah and the One God within Valeron, to help counsel the king on matters of faith and justice. This also led to the setting up of the inquisition courts and prisons. It was a time when the corrupt noble families grew insular and fearful, as they had many secrets that they did not desire to be brought to light.

This period was also witness to a new and successful military campaign. The Church launched a southern crusade into Perova, finally claiming those lands from the current vampire lord – with the final victory coming as the capital of Perova was put to the torch by zealous inquisitors. One more threat had been eradicated and the expansive lands to the south were added to the Kingdom of Valeron. The Church duly claimed its credit by exacting a tithe on the populace.

A Tale of Two Princes
Despite the efforts of the inquisition, magic still remained pervasive in many areas of Valeron society, especially in scholarly circles and within the nobility. In other lands, such as Khitesh, Sargassi and Venetia, magic was not seen as taboo and great advances had already taken place in regards to understanding and mastering the art. Valeron had witnessed the power of such a force during the first crusade, when it was employed against them by Mordland. Such events were not easily forgotten.

During the reigns of King Mendore and King Artemis, there was a gradual and subtle shifting towards an interest in magic. Artemis' youngest son, Fynn, proved a keen scholar and financed a number of excursions into dwarven ruins. Such delves were becoming a popular pastime for treasure seekers and adventurers, as the abandoned tunnels and vaults contained many runic treasures and knowledge of the arcane. These places were dangerous, infested with creatures of the underworld, but the rewards far outweighed the risks. Many runeforged items were now finding their way more frequently into society – and their worth could not be denied when turned against Valeron's foes. Skardland raids were becoming common in the north, troll and goblin raids from the south. Even the goblins were starting to exhibit a greater social structure, with shamans uniting and leading these bands, themselves wielding powerful elemental magics. The inquisitors were always few in number and the physical cost of inscribing sermons of light made holy weapons and armour a rarity. It was becoming clear that, despite the dangers, there was a benefit to understanding this magic rather than living in ignorance.

Fynn proved one of many influential individuals to make runelore more accessible, recovering many records and artefacts from the time of the dwarves, and publishing his findings. The Church was slowly encouraged to take a more lenient attitude towards those who practised such arts. When Fynn's brother, Taul, became king, a chance encounter would further cement this change in stance.

A Khitesh prince, Hussam Ibn al-Aydin, was taking a tour of the southern towns and cities of Valeron. In Greyspire, there was some altercation with inquisitors and city watch, and Hussam and his party were arrested and imprisoned. When word got to Taul, he immediately acted to release the prince – fearing reprisal from Khitesh. He invited Hussam to his court, where the two were to become firm friends. Hussam knew much of the magical arts having studied and graduated from the House of Wisdom in Khitesh, which trained mages to control their powers. Indeed, the sand schooners that plied the Dune Seas were powered by air magic – enabling them to traverse the expansive deserts with ease.

With Hassam's help, Taul set up the first collage of magic in Assay. Although there was opposition from the Church, Taul used his authority as king to push for its inception, to give magic a more respectable standing in society. Later, in the reign of Taul's son, the University of Magic was set up in Talanost, which already had a thriving academic culture. By now, the Church had lost much of its former influence on society, with magic now rising in ascendency. These two would always remain uneasy bedfellows, however, when times called for heroes – these rivalries had to be pushed aside for the greater good. And one of those tests was fast approaching.

The Legion of Shadow

Whilst Valeron was riven with civil war during the War of the Princes, far to the south – in the desert lands of Khitesh – a remarkable event had taken place. Travellers from another world had finally made the dangerous voyage through the Shroud to arrive on Dormus. These were the elves, a tall insectoid race that had a command of alien magics and machinery, the likes of which had not been seen before on Dormus. Their pyramid structures appeared across the deserts, having being pulled through the Shroud by the powerful magnetic energies of their lodestones. These strange artefacts were crafted from magnetite, a metal that had been common on their own home world of Logum. Strong in magnetic energies, this metal was the reason their world was doomed to an inescapable fate – to be pulled into the core of their own sun. Hence, the elves had been locked in a battle against time to save themselves from annihilation. Thanks to their ingenuity, they had succeeded, and now found themselves on Dormus.

The elves and the Khiteshi remained at odds for many hundreds of years – the elves being reclusive and contemptuous of the lesser races they now shared a world with. Magnetite was their most precious resource and the deserts of Khitesh proved lacking in such provision. Mistakenly assuming all of Dormus was a similar desert wasteland, the elves started to look elsewhere once again. They constructed a gate – a more advanced amalgamation of their past technology and magic – and managed to attune it to the presence of another world. That world was the shadow realm of Umbril, now enslaved by demons. When the portal was activated and the first elves took their daring step through into the unknown, little did they know that they had sealed their own doom. What they discovered on the other side was a world that had long since fallen to Aisa and her demons. Before the portal could be deactivated, these dark and twisted creations started to pour through the gateway – and so began the Shadow War.

The demons and their mortal agents fell on their enemies with brutal abandon. Like a swarm of locusts, these barbaric forces swept northwards, destroying everything in their wake. The enmity between the elves and the Khiteshi meant that they were unable to put aside their differences and form a solid coalition. Khitesh was devastated, its once prosperous cities reduced to smoking ruins – its people scattered across the deserts. The elves were entirely wiped out, their race now considered extinct. Far from content with such victories, the demon legion pushed northwards into what had been old Perova, sacking towns and cities on their endless rampage.

If such a force remained unchecked, then Valeron would inevitably fall. A great army was mustered under King Samuel and – for the first time – this force included those skilled in the magic arts. These mighty mages would be fighting side-by-side with the faithful of the Church – their rivalries had to be forgotten if humanity was to be saved.

At Talanost, the two armies came together and there were many bloody and desperate engagements. The magic of the Talanost mages would prove pivotal in the war, helping to turn the tide of many battles. Such a clash of magical forces left the region devastated and barren, riven with magical anomalies that, even to this day, remain a danger to the unwary across the desolation of the Bone Fields.

The war was finally brought to a conclusion thanks to a courageous band of Khiteshi and Valeron archmages. They were able to locate the source of the incursion and close the gateway. This portal, which became known as the Shadow Gate, was then moved to the University of Magic in Talanost for protection and further study. One of the archmages responsible for this victory was a young man named Avian Dale. He would later become a close advisor to the kings of Valeron – his seemingly unageing appearance and immortality leading to much speculation over his true origin and powers.

The losses had been great, but the legion had finally been defeated. Grudgingly, the Church was forced to accept that magic had played a vital role in the victory. Following the Shadow War, the psychological impact of what had happened started to take its toll on the populace. They had never been threatened in such a way before by an otherworldly force. If such things could exist, was there worse horrors out there – and who would protect them? Fear and superstition became rife, and the Church once again found itself struggling to bolster people's faith in the One God.

Before he died, Samuel moved the royal residences back to Assay. This was a further blow to the Church – who had formerly enjoyed the privilege of the king's presence in the city of Solace, which had always been considered the heart of the Church since the days of King Hemides.

Saint Allam the Prophet

In the two hundred or more years since the peace agreement between Valeron and Mordland had ended, the latter power had again been growing in strength. The islands of Veda had finally come fully under their control and the new khan, Kush Zayat, now took on the mantle of emperor. His armies started to push once again into the contested lands – and started to build settlements on the eastern steppes, which would become known as Gorgatha and Shinar.

Another tentative agreement was made between the two forces to avoid any renewal of hostilities. Valeron recognised those territories that Mordland had claimed. The treaty was sealed with a marriage, between the king of Valeron and one of the emperor's daughters. This was a ruse by the emperor – his daughter was to act as a spy, being a powerful sorceress in her own right. The king fully suspected the deception and treated her cruelly. In the end, she murdered the king in cold blood – and both her and her son, Sable, were imprisoned. Such events inevitably led once more to war and another crusade to beat back Mordland from the contested lands.

In the year 1184 of the Ascension, King Gerard came to the throne, inheriting debt from his predecessors and a crusade in the east that had ground to an indecisive halt. He was losing support and there were murmurings that his bloodline was weak and his leadership lacking. Both himself and the Church were in desperate need of some twist of fate to change their beleaguered fortunes and galvanise support once again. Luckily, the king's youngest son, Allam, was to be that twist of fate.

His young son had been plagued by visions since an infant. These had largely been dismissed by his father for fear of bringing further shame on his reign. However, after one particularly violent seizure, Allam insisted that he had been gifted a vision from the One God – that there was a light in the west, a holy artefact that was calling him. Initially sceptical, King Gerard was gradually persuaded by the clergy that this could be turned into a boon to change both their fortunes. By declaring a new crusade, led by a holy prophet and guided by the One God, the populace might at last be given renewed faith and hope in both the Church and the monarchy.

Gerard ordered the crusade, mustering his finest knights, soldiers and dedicated inquisitors, to accompany Allam into the far west. These lands had always remained wild and somewhat untameable, with Wiccan tribes laying ancestral claim to much of the region, and only a few small towns and villages scraping out a meagre existence amongst the stagnant fenlands. It was not a region that Valeron had shown any great interest in before, but now it was to become a new theatre of war.

Driven by his strange visions, Allam led his forces into the west to fulfil his calling. Such a journey inevitably led to contact and skirmishes with the Wiccan. Allam implored both sides to reach a peaceable outcome – for he only desired passage westwards to seek the light that drew him. Unfortunately, others within his army had other agendas and such meetings would inevitably end with hostility and bloodshed.

The Wiccan lands were gradually lost to blade and torch as Allam's forces pushed ever westwards. Word of his many triumphs spread throughout Valeron, making Allam a national hero. Some even spoke of him in the same breath as Judah, seeing him as the true second coming of the One God's divine light.

His many adventures became the stuff of legend and ballad, painting a saintly picture of the prophet and his gallant knights. The reality was significantly bloodier and more barbarous, as the Wiccans fought desperately for their lands. Outmatched by the military strength arrayed against them, they had little choice but to seek refuge in the deeper woods and remote hills, giving up what fertile land they once enjoyed. Valeron had driven its banner deeply into this region and was not letting go of it.

The story of Allam was to have a tragic ending. His visions had finally led him southwards, in pursuit of a holy object that was purported to be the key to finding the light that he was seeking. He was travelling with only his closest knights and disciples when they were set upon by trolls. The battle has been retold many times and with many variations. The most popular, allegedly recorded by a survivor of that battle, speaks of the trolls hardening their skin to stone. The knight's blades were of no use against such hardy protection. Allam prayed to the One God, then ordered his company of knights to throw down their swords and put faith in their god. As they did so, holy light wrapped around their fists, gifting them divine strength. Empowered by this strange enchantment, the knights were able to fight back, smashing through the ranks of trolls. However, they were unable to turn the tide of battle – instead they made a valiant last stand. Allam and his trusted knights were later sainted, joining Davius Glint and others who had valiantly fought and died for the One God.

A year later, Gerard and his only remaining son met with an accident whilst on a hunting trip, leaving the way open for his cousin and devout church man, Justinius, to take over the throne. He immediately renewed efforts in the west, determined not to lose any of the land gained through Allam's crusade. Now known as 'The Holy Lands', Justinius claimed these for the One God and denounced the pagan tribes who sought to oppose such progress. The newly-conquered region would later become a popular destination for pilgrims, eager to visit the church in Carvel dedicated to Saint Allam.

Rise of the Cardinal

Nearly two hundred years have passed since Allam's martyrdom. In that time, the contested lands to the east have become little more than a ruined wasteland of crumbling garrisons and spirit-haunted ruins. Mordland still dominates the eastern steppes and occasionally launches raids further west, but their current emperor appears to have set his gaze elsewhere, having coerced both the nations of Vaidskrig and Sargassi into the empire, and pushing this new naval strength eastwards across the unchartered seas.

The Church maintains a presence in the contested lands, with its bravest crusaders forever seeking to eliminate the demons and other creatures that now freely stalk the land. Antioch in particular, remains a city that the Church is eager to reclaim – now a hunting ground for all kinds of monsters drawn from the plagued wilderness.

The recent murders of King Leonidas and his only surviving son, Malden, has left Valeron without an heir. A regent has now been appointed until a suitable replacement can be approved. This regent is a representative of the Church – Cardinal Rile – a close advisor to the ailing and now largely ineffectual leaders, Lord and Lady Justice. Rile's sudden rise to power is steeped in controversy and suspicion. The deaths of the King and his son, Malden, have been blamed on Mordland agents eager to destabilise Valeron in preparation for an invasion. However, there are others that have come to question the serious lack of compelling evidence – leaving some to wonder if Rile himself was behind the murders to place himself in power.

His influence is already being felt. The Council of Nine in Assay has been temporarily suspended with no explanation – and the mages have been refused finance to rebuild the University in Talanost, destroyed during the second and brief incursion of the Legion of Shadow. The Church would appear to be on the ascendency once again – with those practising the magical arts now fearing reprisal and judgement.

The Holy Orders of the One God

Throughout the ages, the Church has furthered its knowledge and skills in wielding the divine light. Based on the teachings of their holy messenger, Judah, and the efforts of his angels during those early missionary tours, the Church was granted an orderly structure, which has largely been adhered to through times of peace and war. This structure has expanded as time has gone on, to now encompass a number of different orders. Each has a role to play in furthering the Church's aims across the Kingdom of Valeron and beyond.

Lord and Lady Justice: The heads of the Church are Lord and Lady Justice, who are democratically voted into their position by the leading members of the clergy. This is a position that is held for life, which has caused some tension and frustration as the current Lord and Lady Justice are both now over 150 years old. Many are starting to wonder if there is more than faith and divine spirit keeping them alive. Despite their apparent longevity, both are frail and weak, and their minds often clouded by confusion. This has meant that their closest advisor, Cardinal Rile, has been able to dominate them both – and finally gain himself the throne of Valeron.

The Inquisition: Many rightly fear the sight of an inquisitor, resplendent in their plated armour and white cloaks. Since their inception, these mighty warriors have represented the righteous justice of the Church, having powers to arrest and question those that they deem suspicious of treasonous acts. They operate out of Durnhollow, a vast stone fortress in the western mountains that was once dwarven, but now pressed into the service of the Church. Here, inquisitors take those they wish to put to the question, using their powers to reveal the insidious lies and secrets of their victim, and steadily unveiling the many plots and factions that pose a threat to the righteous.

The Cardinals: The head of each church or cathedral is known as a bishop. After serving in this role for several decades or more, a bishop may be recommended to become a cardinal. These are the highest-ranking members of the clergy – usually based at the White Abbey in Solace, where they help govern the Church's affairs. Cardinals will also tour the cathedrals and churches around Valeron, giving rousing speeches to help encourage congregations, and using their divine powers to heal the sick. Their order is visibly denoted by the long red robes that they wear, which symbolise the blood they are willing to shed in the One God's name. They also wear the symbol of a white rose, to reflect their piety and pureness.

The White Abbots: The most powerful wielders of the divine light, these men and women are trained from an early age in the arts of inscription. By adulthood, they will already have learned the intricate techniques and prayerful rituals required to channel their inner kha into the sermons of light that can empower flesh and iron. Each time they engrave such scripture, they expend some of their own life force, which can never be recovered. Hence, most abbots are sickly and frail, gradually sacrificing all of their vigor as they bless the weapons and warriors of the faith.

The Holy Martyrs: The angel Eglantine Pugh discovered a new application of the divine light through a series of visions before her death. These new sermons, of which she was granted knowledge, could be inscribed onto the flesh of a holy individual to gradually turn their blood into a healing tonic. These priests, known as martyrs, have strict lives of

prayer, ritual and abstinence, to ensure the continued purity of their blood. Every month, they leech themselves of this precious essence. When combined with other secret reagents, the healing properties of these tonics is said to be incredibly potent, instantly sealing wounds and knitting broken bones faster than any other healing magic. Sadly, these tonics have yet to prove effective in healing the abbots.

The Paladins: Only the greatest holy warriors get the rare opportunity to receive a full baptism and transform themselves into holy avatars. This gruelling ritual involves their entire body, save the face, undergoing scriptural carving. It is not unknown for several abbots to give their lives in the creation of a paladin, due to the hundreds of sermons that are inscribed into the flesh. Some paladins even choose the final agony-inducing sacrifice of having their eyeballs inscribed. This grants them perfect night vision, although such a sacrifice means they can never sleep again. Once the ritual is completed, a paladin is literally a glowing embodiment of the divine light, blessed with superhuman strength, and capable of single-handedly taking on a whole mob of enemies. However, due to the sheer human cost of creating such a body, paladins remain incredibly rare – but highly revered as true heroes of the realm.

The Witchfinders: Founded by the famed hunter, Jasper Crane, the order of witchfinders serve as holy watchmen, often operating alone or with an apprentice, to hunt down witches, demons, vampires and other creatures of the dark. They are well-versed in monster-lore and will always carry a multitude of weapons, charms and other trinkets designed to weaken and take down their prey. Nearly all witchfinders train at the Acorlidge in Greyspire, where they learn the arts of blade and flintlock – the latter a recent addition to their versatile armoury, but one that has proven exceptionally effective in evening the odds against powerful spellcasters.

The Crusaders and Templars: Davius Glint effectively became the original divine warrior, when Judah inscribed his blade with the first sermon of light. This holy champion was later sainted and positioned as the figurehead for a new order of holy knights. These skilled swordsmen, known as crusaders, wielded armaments blessed with smiting and protection, making them a stalwart addition to regular battalions – and capable of going toe-to-toe with demons and other nefarious opponents. Later, during the reign of King Samuel, some crusaders were initiated into a separate order known as the Knights Templar. These venerated warriors were often tasked with delicate diplomatic missions, often in other countries and regions of Dormus. To this end, they are typically well-versed in languages and cultures, and have the ability to seamlessly shift from imposing warrior to elusive spy at a moment's notice. Today, the templars still operate around Dormus, although – as always – their missions and objectives remain shrouded in mystery.

The Holy Fist: Inspired by Saint Allam's final stand, when he blessed his warriors' fists with light, a new arm of the Church was brought into being – holding to the belief that the holy word and the divine light are the only weapons a devout warrior should wield. This belief became firmly grounded in the monasteries around Valeron, where previously meditative recluses of faith now embraced a new training regime to uphold Allam's legacy. These devout followers inscribed their fists with hallowed sermons, whilst training both mind and body to master the techniques of Hun-Bo, a dervish-style combat art from the desert regions of Khitesh. These fighting monks follow a doctrine of peace, but if others ever foolishly threaten such harmony, then these zealous warriors have no qualms in proving the deadly superiority of their expert skills.

5
Timeline of Dormus

The great cosmic being, Yu'Weh, dreams of life – and from him the first two Fates are created, Gabriel and Kismet. The union of these Fates creates a third, Aisa. Forever trapped in an endless sleep, Yu'Weh impresses his purpose on his three servants – to create nine worlds and fill them with life. Kismet is the spinner who creates the weave, the web of creation. Gabriel fills its strands with destiny, being the only one to know the true outcome of the plan. Aisa is the ender, who brings death at its appointed time – each severed essence returning to its source to be reborn again.

Age of Awakening
Kismet, one of the three celestial Fates, crafts the world of Dormus. Its prime element is fire. Out of all the elder races, only the dwarves are

able to survive on this volcanic world. They dig deep into the depths of the underworld to escape the insufferable surface temperatures.

- The youngest Fate, Aisa rebels. Millions of lives are cut short as she attacks the cosmic weave in an effort to destroy the grand plan.
- Left with no choice, the Fates wage war with each other. Aisa is defeated and shackled in a prison known as Hel.
- Aisa creates the Shroud, a maelstrom of chaos that seeks to engulf the nine worlds. She births the first demons, who are able to wield the chaotic forces of the Shroud – channelling them into powerful magics.
- Corrupted by Aisa's essence, Kismet starts to create imperfections in the weave. The lesser races are born in their multitudes, many bestial and chaotic.

Age of Strife

The dwarven underground cities are overwhelmed by an endless tide of goblins, trolls and other creatures spawned by Kismet's corruption. Unable to defend their homes, the dwarves escape into the deeper tunnels and caverns.

- The beleaguered dwarves discover the existence of the titans – a mysterious race of giants fashioned from earth and stone. These giants are blessed with a deep wisdom and understanding of magic.
- The titans share their knowledge of runelore with the dwarves, showing them the rituals and sigils required to summon elementals from the Shroud and bind them to weapons and armour.
- With the aid of their newly-learned runecraft, the dwarves fight back and reclaim their cities from the lesser races.

Age of Discovery

The titans continue to instruct the dwarves on the ways of magic. The dwarves become expert at crafting runeworked weapons and armour – and begin to master geomancy, allowing them to abandon their picks and shovels, and sculpt their underground cities with the power of magic.

- Kismet turns her gaze to the world of Dormus and realises her mistake in its hasty creation. She channels her powers of earth and water into the fabric of Dormus.
- Water cools the heat of this volcanic world. Leylines spread their life-giving energies, helping plants flourish in the mineral-rich soils.
- The first humans are born to Dormus. Whilst proving highly adaptable, they struggle in their efforts to defend themselves from the marauding tribes of goblins, giants and other creatures that have been forced to the surface by the dwarves.

Age of Sundering
A rift tears open deep within Dormus, providing a gateway for demons and elementals from the Shroud to spill into the underworld. The dwarven cities once again come under attack. Many fall to the demonic invasion, whilst others are able to fight back with their magics and runed armaments. A bitter war ensues between the dwarves and the demons.

- Many decades of fierce warfare force the dwarves to reorganise their social structure, forming a rigid military and magic division within each city. The aim is to better manage their particular strengths in order to beat back the invasion.
- Demons reach the surface world and come into conflict with humans. The latter do not have the weapons or magic to adequately defend themselves. Many tribes are wiped out in the ensuing confrontations. Survivors seek refuge within the underground dwarven cities.
- The dwarves teach humans some of the secrets of their runelore and magic, to better equip them in their wars against the demons. In the southern jungles, these tribes erect great temples and ziggurats under powerful leaders. These people call themselves the Lamuri.
- As the invasion intensifies, the military faction of dwarves begins to dabble in blood rituals and magic, forging pacts

with traitorous demon lords in order to gain an upper hand in the struggle.

The Dark Ages

The dwarves are finally able to collapse the tunnels around the rift and stop the invasion. However, they have paid a huge cost. Many of their cities lie in ruin and for those that survive, their addiction to magic has left them forever changed.

- The Dours, a faction of the dwarves that have willingly given in to their demonic powers, now seek to conquer the surface world. Their underground cities have become a shadow of their former glory. They set about erecting great cities and fortresses in the world above.
- A civil war breaks out between the Dours and the Illumanti – an opposing faction of dwarves devoted to upholding the original ideals of their society. They endeavour to aid the humans against the Dour expansion.
- For hundreds of years, the dwarves are trapped in a bitter struggle with each other. The Dours grow ever more enslaved to their demonic masters, all trace of their original beliefs and values lost.
- Under the influence of the Illumanti, the humans start to organise themselves into larger tribal groups ruled by a king. These scattered kingdoms start to expand their territories, bringing them into regular conflict with each other.
- Following a terrible cataclysm that leaves great jagged rifts across northern Dormus, a powerful archdemon is released. Once a mortal seeking power to save his people, this powerful entity is now enslaved by a demonic weapon known as Ragnarok. Seemingly unstoppable, his great army marches south, destroying much of the Lamuri civilisation – and finally, after a titanic battle, is defeated in the dwarven city of Tartarus.

The Rise of Man

Centuries of war has decimated the dwarven civilisation. Despite being a long-lived and hardy race, the dwarves are not as prolific as humans, nor are they able to adapt quickly to the ever-changing environment.

- Scholars still argue over the cause of the dwarven extinction. Some say that a virulent disease was the final blow to an already decimated people, others believe the wars left them so few in number that they had no chance of adequately recovering. A later theory, and one that is gaining traction, is that the last of the dwarves abandoned everything and went deeper into the underworld, cutting themselves off from all contact with the surface. If so, then the fate of those dwarves remains unknown.
- After beating back tribes of goblins, giants and other creatures, many human kingdoms start to establish themselves. During this period, the Kingdom of Valeron rises to prominence under its fearsome king and warmaker, Magnus Valeron.
- Some humans remain as nomadic tribes, preferring the freedom of the wilds to the cramped confines of towns and villages. These tribes, often referred to collectively as the Wiccan, forge a strong bond with the dryad groves of the deep woods.

The Ages of Wisdom and Woe
In the southern lands of Dormus, a group of seven mysterious travellers emerge from the desert, bringing advanced knowledge of astronomy, engineering, farming and religion to the nomadic tribes. The great civilisation known as Khitesh is born.

- Ruled by a leader known as a sultan, Khitesh become a thriving hub of enlightenment and learning. These new discoveries slowly spread northwards into the other kingdoms.
- Valeron wages war on its rivals, the Amaral to the west and the Franks to the east. Amaral is conquered, but Franklin stubbornly resists Valeron's expansion.
- The tribes of Mordland are united under a khan and invade Franklin, devastating the kingdom. Valeron does not aid its neighbour due to other threats to its lands – from Perova to the south and Vaidskrig pirates from the north.

- The Mordland khan is finally defeated and the army routed due to in-fighting between its tribes. The Frankish king and his son lose their lives during the campaign.
- With no heir, Franklin is left weak and largely defenceless. Valeron claims what remains of its shattered lands in return for allowing the surviving city of Lull to have its own nominated governor.

Judah the Lightbringer

The celestial Fate, Gabriel, weakened and blind by his former battle with Aisa, sacrifices himself to the celestial weave – his essence filling each and every strand of life with a measure of his divine light. One of these strands, infused with the last of Gabriel's strength, becomes a great prophet and messiah. His name is Judah.

- Judah appears to his seven apostles at the coastal town of Crowfoot (later to be renamed Hope's Light). He begins a ministry tour of the towns and villages of Valeron, preaching the word of the One God.
- Judah wins over the king of Valeron and escapes execution. He goes east into the broken lands of Franklin and founds the holy city of Antioch – planting his rod at its centre and summoning a citadel of celestial light known as 'The Divine Vigil'.
- Judah grants his seven apostles divine powers, turning them into angels. He sends them forth to spread the word of the One God throughout Dormus.
- Judah and his companion, Davius Glint, are captured by a Mordland army. The khan mocks Judah and his message of a One God. Judah is crucified on a Mordland cross.
- As Judah dies, he ascends as an archangel – and releases a mighty blast of divine force that decimates the entire Mordland army. Only the loyal knight, Davius Glint, survives. He brings word of Judah's sacrifice to the people.

Age of Enlightenment (Year 1-226 of the Ascension)

Valeron enters an age of enlightenment. Judah's seven angels conduct their missionary tours, spreading the teachings of the One God throughout Dormus.

- The angel, Erastus Dain, is given inspired visions that lead to the creation of the first cathedrals and churches to the One God. The cathedrals are works of wonder, drawing travellers and pilgrims from all over Dormus.
- Skardland raiders find a navigable route through the mountain passes and start to raid northern Valeron. Davius Glint dies valiantly in battle and is sainted.
- The angels record their inspired visions and sermons in a set of books, which would later be known as The Apocryphal Texts. Several angels leave Valeron to take their word to other nations. Mary Malley and Timon Fray are never heard of again.
- The last known angel, Timothy Sawyer, dies at the age of 244.
- The south lands of Perova fall under the sway of a vampire lord, who enslaves the populace through a demonic tome uncovered from a Dour stronghold.
- Mordland forms an alliance with the Vaidskrig and raids the islands of Veda. The Mordland leader, Altan Khutala, discovers the Vedic texts that hold dark secrets of the arcane.

The First Crusade (Year 227-277 of the Ascension)
Mordland has regained its strength and launches an invasion into Valeron. With a fast and mobile army, and mastery of dark sorcery, Mordland lays waste to all in its path.

- King Metrias of Valeron calls for a holy crusade to take back the contested lands. The Order of Davius is founded and its knights become the first crusaders.
- Antioch changes hands many times over a prolonged war that lasts nearly fifty years.
- The Mordland army pushes further westwards into central Valeron. However, starvation and disease, as well as weakening morale, slow their advance. One of the Mordland generals takes matters into his own hands and assassinates Altan Khutala.

- A peace treaty is signed between the nations of Valeron and Mordland, that will last one hundred years.

The Witch Hunts (Year 278-362 of the Ascension)
Famine and rebellion spread across a battle-weary Valeron – a country now riddled with discontent. Magic and pagan worship are on the rise as people desperately seek comfort and empowerment in these dark days.

- Before his death, Metrias sets up the inquisition, to try and reassert the Church's authority by rooting out rebels and sinners.
- Metrias' only heir dies of a wasting disease. Valeron is plunged further into chaos. Several contenders vie for the throne. This conflict would become known as 'The War of the Princes'.
- Hemides, a war hero and bishop, finally wins the throne with the Church's backing. He immediately sets about bringing order to a ravaged country.
- Witch hunts take place across Valeron as inquisitors and witchfinders seek to bring an end to pagan worship and the practice of dangerous magics.
- In Khitesh an otherworldly race known as the elves arrive on Dormus. Initial contact with the Khiteshi does not go well and the two become rivals.

Magic and Lost Treasures (Year 363-494 of the Ascension)
The Church is striving to usher in a golden age of faith and righteousness. However, magic and demon worship are still rife around Dormus – and the discovery of ancient treasures only serves to further people's interest in the arcane.

- The newly appointed king, Bevan, sets up the offices of Lord and Lady Justice to counsel future Valeron kings on matters of faith and justice. The inquisition set up their dungeons in Durnhollow to imprison and question the unrighteous.
- Valeron launches a campaign into Perova to liberate its enslaved populace from the line of vampires that has

dominated the land. The campaign is successful and the capital of Perova is burned to the ground by the inquisition.

- Explorers and hunters start to forge west. Contact is made with the Halli of the prairie lands and the numerous tribes of the Terral Jungle. Ruins of the Lamuri civilisation are found – as well as many dwarven cities. Tales of these exotic discoveries and daring expeditions spread throughout Valeron.
- Following Bevan's death, his successor and those that follow, are less disposed towards the Church and prove more open to the arcane discoveries that are taking place around Dormus. Whilst the Church is intent on silencing much of the esoteric knowledge that is coming to light, these kings – including Mendore, Artemis and Taul – push for greater study and understanding of the arcane.
- Taul's successor, King Wynne, sets up the University of Magic in the former-Perovan city of Talanost. This centre of study, along with the colleges now appearing in the other major cities, offer a safe haven for those with the wealth and privilege to practise their magical arts.

The Shadow War (Year 495-550 of the Ascension)
The elves create a portal to the shadow realm of Umbril. They had hoped to discover fresh resources and knowledge – instead they inadvertently unleash a demonic army on the world, known as the Legion of Shadow.

- The legion invades the desert lands of Khitesh. The elves and the Khiteshi fail to overcome their bitter rivalry and both are brought to ruin.
- The demons forge north, rampaging through the Badlands and into what was once Perova. Towns and cities are devastated by their relentless fury.
- At Talanost, the Valeron king, Samuel, is able to bring the full force of his army to bear against the demons. With the aid of noble crusaders and Talanost mages, the army is able to finally defeat the legion and reclaim Talanost.
- A coalition of Khiteshi and Valeron archmages successfully venture south into the deserts to locate and close the shadow

gate. This ends the Shadow War. The gate is later moved to the city of Talanost for study and protection.
- The legion were masters of shadow magic. Many mages and treasure hunters pillage the battlegrounds for tomes and artefacts from Umbril – hoping to further their understanding of this magic and the world that it comes from.
- Many human agents of the legion escape into the wilds. Branded with the mark of their demon overlord, Shimaza, these devoted followers are blessed with immortality and potent powers. Known as the Neverin, these 'shadowborn' continue to further their master's plans – hoping one day to have their revenge.
- The great civilisation of Khitesh lies in shattered ruins. It will take many hundreds of years for its people to rebuild and gain some semblance of their former glory.

Treason and Betrayal (Year 551-1184 of the Ascension)
Mordland once again rises up as a world power, seeking to claim lands for its newly proclaimed emperor. This long and harrowing period sees Valeron locked in a succession of wars with Mordland, that leave the contested lands a ruined hellscape of crumbling ruins and haunted battlefields.

- Mordland settles on the eastern steppes of the Contested Lands, building the fortified settlements of Shinar and Gorgatha. Valeron – still recovering from the Shadow War – grudgingly accepts this encroachment. A further agreement of peace is made, which is sealed with the marriage of one of the emperor's daughters to the Valeron king, Holbein.
- The king's new wife is a spy for Mordland and a sorceress. Her cruel treatment at the hands of her brutish husband leads to his murder. Both the widowed queen and her only son are found guilty and imprisoned as traitors. They later escape and find passage north into the frozen reaches of Skardland.
- The king's murder and the queen's imprisonment inevitably led to fresh hostilities between Mordland and Valeron. Many

crusades are launched during this period, but none garner any gains or glory.

- Skardland raids resume in the north. King Remis puts a controversial plan into motion to build a vast fortified wall across the northern plains. This ambitious project takes nearly a decade to complete and becomes known as Bitter Keep – more for its cost in coin and human life, than the bleak lands that it guards.

Allam the Prophet (Year 1184-1252 of the Ascension)

Crippled with war debt and a rebellious populace, Valeron teeters on the brink of collapse. King Gerard lacks the support of the people and the Church's influence is waning after the failure of its many crusades. However, the king's youngest son offers a new hope – a figurehead for the people to rally behind. Allam claims to be a prophet of the One God and has received divine visions of a 'light' in the west. A campaign is launched to help Allam seek out the meaning of these visions.

- Accompanied by an army of knights and soldiers, Allam pushes westwards. He preaches peace and understanding between Valeron and the Wiccan people, but his words fall on deaf ears.
- Many of the Wiccan are forced from their ancestral lands, refusing to bend the knee to a foreign king. This seeds a sour enmity between the two factions, which continues to this day.
- Allam becomes obsessed by his visions – believing the 'light' to be a holy relic that will usher in a new age of enlightenment. Sadly, his quest is cut short when his party is set upon by powerful adversaries and Allam is killed. Allam and his knights are sainted by the Church.
- A new king comes to the throne – Justinius. He immediately seeks to capitalise on Allam's gains by sending fresh troops to conquer and hold the western reaches.
- All of the Wiccan lands are claimed by the king. The region is renamed 'The Holy Lands' and becomes a centre for pilgrimage and worship.

Rise of the Empire (Year 1253-1383 of the Ascension)

Despite its recent western expansion, Valeron has invariably turned inwards, its kings more focused on consolidation rather than conquest. Meanwhile, Mordland is now expanding. A new and vigorous young emperor has brought fresh impetus to what had become a stagnant nation. With new allies at his side, the emperor has set his sights on the east – and its vast unchartered seas.

- Queen Shade Aboola consents to making Sargassi a member of the Mordland empire – an arrangement that brings mutual benefit to both parties. Aboola craves greater mastery of her magical powers – and now consorts with Mordland sorcerers to unlock such gifts. In return, Mordland has been given access to the water-logged caverns of the southern jungles. These have proved a rich hunting ground for the seraphine crystals that are vital in the manufacture of sparkpowder.
- The High Carl of Vaidskrig has entered into a similar arrangement with Mordland, albeit one that the carls of the islands are not happy with. Great wealth has been afforded them in exchange for their ships and talented sailors – but things may be set to turn sour, as the Vaidskrig are a fierce and independent people who are not easily cowed.
- Earthquakes in the northern regions have become more common, particularly in the area of Skardland. The current Drokke of the tribes, Skoll Frostgrieve, is purported to be missing, leaving the Skards weakened and leaderless.

The End Days (1384-present day)

There are some who claim that Dormus has entered the end days, as prophesised by Judah and recorded in the penultimate book of scriptures. He spoke at length of great earthquakes and a great calamity – the birth pains that would herald in a time of darkness when evil would be on the ascendancy. Only a righteous few would survive through these critical times to help guide Dormus to its true destiny...

- A shadowborn sorcerer known as Zul Ator manages to reactivate the shadow gate in Talanost, leading to a second invasion by the Legion of Shadow. The mages of the university are quick to react and create a shield around the city to entrap the demons.

- General Ravenwing of the Valeron army leads a spirited campaign to defeat the legion and reclaim the ruined city. It is rumoured that a shadowborn traitor aided the general and was key to the legion's downfall – but their identity remains a mystery.

- In the west, the Wiccan are uniting under a new leader, Conall the Crow King. He seeks retribution for the wrongs that have been wrought on his people over the past centuries. While lacking in numbers, Conall's forces have a strong affinity with nature magic, and many of their weapons and armour carry dryad enchantments. He believes his victory has been prophesied, and now leads his people on a barbarous rampage across Valeron.

- The king's youngest son, Arran, is sent west to Salton, to reinforce the garrison with fresh troops. He has not been heard of since and it is assumed his retinue was ambushed and all were killed.

- In the north, a terrible demonic beast named Jormungdar was released from the depths of the underworld. The seismic upheaval caused by its arrival has led to huge rifts and fissures splitting across areas of northern Valeron. It is rumoured a strange wanderer who calls himself the Ghost Prince, has united the disparate Skardland tribes – and under his leadership, they were able to defeat the gigantic demon before it could gain its full strength.

- Valeron's king, Leonidas and his only surviving son, Malden, were murdered in their beds. It is believed that Mordland is to blame, but others around court are less convinced by such claims. Cardinal Rile, the advisor to Lord and Lady Justice, is now acting as regent until a suitable candidate is found for the throne.

6
Factions of Valeron

Valeron is a kingdom divided. Through its many conquests, it has always sought to expand and absorb the many peoples and cultures of the continent. As it has done so, Valeron has ruthlessly tried to impose its own faith and ideals on these newly acquired citizens. However, such a dogmatic and expansionist attitude has only brought more problems, as society splinters into many fractious groups – and those that Valeron seeks to dominate and oppress, become galvanised in opposition. The wealth of the kingdom is becoming ever more polarised, with the rich able to dominate the poor, and those with the access to power and knowledge having the upper hand over those who remain in ignorance.

Many monsters roam the lands, from lowly goblins to wild elementals, but some will say these are not the real threat – not the real enemies. In these dark days, eyes can easily turn to friends and neighbours, and to the stranger on the street. Suspicion and distrust are rife, and loyalty is not something easily won or freely given. Nevertheless, there are those that do find some common bond and identity – perhaps through a shared culture, belief or even persecution. These factions find strength in shared values and aims, and a desire to protect that which they have earned, which can so easily be taken away. In these troubled times, some will rise and others will fall, there will be victors and there will be losers, and there will certainly be conflict. Whether Valeron can find the unity it needs to strengthen itself for the challenges ahead is still unknown. More likely, the kingdom may slip ever closer to division, revolution and war.

The Alchemical and Botany Society

Alchemy has always, in some shape or form, been a part of human society. Even mankind's earliest ancestors looked to the plants and other reagents of the natural world for properties that could heal the sick or bring relief to suffering. Overtime, this science of mixing components to craft potions, ointments and remedies, has been recorded and expanded upon as new species of flora and fauna have been discovered, and their alchemical merits catalogued.

With the rise of the Church and its healing arts, such tonics were seen as the workings of pagan magic. Those of faith would shun such remedies in favour of the curative arts of the acolytes and priests. But alchemy continued to be a fast-growing science and one that had many applications for daily life. Unlike magic that could be volatile and dangerous, alchemy had accepted rules – and results could be reliably replicated with the correct level of skill and components. Therefore, it would be a rare soldier or adventurer who didn't venture out without at least one flask of healing for reassurance.

Overtime, knowledge of the science has increased – with new and more powerful concoctions constantly being discovered. The greatest contributor to this knowledge has been the Alchemical and Botany Society.

The society started as a small conglomerate of like-minded chemists who were keen to share and collate their knowledge. When the University of Magic in Talanost was finally announced and its construction started, the society was asked to be a part of the academic teaching board, to help both educate students in the ways of alchemical lore and also provide a centre for the society to conduct further research.

Sometime, during the reign of King Remis, the society started to expand as a result of its botanical studies in other regions of the land, from the wilds of the Saskat Prairies to the steaming jungles of the south. Their mobile research centres would often end up expanding, becoming small settlements and then villages. One of these was Nautica in the west, which had started as a small expedition to study marine life along the coastline and also the rare plants and fungi of the prairies. Such lands were dangerous, so there was a call for explorers and adventurers to help with the studies. Nautica, despite its remote location, quickly drew settlers – its expansion aided by its prime location on the west coast, where ships could also stop for rest and provision. Eventually, all of the society's studies and experiments were relocated from the university to its outlying expedition centres – and from there, it became structured into what was to become a wide-ranging organisation known as the Alchemical and Botany Society.

No-one is exactly clear on who the society's benefactors are, but over time, the society has expanded to include archaeologists and historians, as well as several renowned mercenary companies. In addition to studying the flora and fauna of the world, the society has also begun exploring ruins and cataloguing its finds. Such actions have often led to controversy, as it has not been unknown for the society to lay claim to certain historic sites, inhibiting others from gaining access. There is even talk that the society, rather than fulfilling their obligation to share their findings with the wider populace, are actually keeping secrets hidden – and many are the rumours of underground vaults where they store their ancient treasures and conduct experiments beyond prying eyes.

Whatever its aims or controversies, the society has proven a boon to adventurers, who are always encouraged to help with expeditions. Often this might involve clearing out monster-infested ruins or providing protection to explorers as they venture into unchartered regions. The pay may not always be equal to the dangers, but the work will always be plentiful for those who don't ask too many questions.

The Arcane Hand

Persecution is nothing new for those who find themselves tainted by the Shroud. Some choose such a life, desiring power and knowledge of the arcane. Others are just victims of chance, often discovering their powers by accident and having little control over how they manifest. Unless born to a wealthy family or one with the right connections, then the chance of getting aid and support is slim. The Church has created a climate of fear within Valeron and few are willing to risk associating with a magic user if it means drawing the attention of a witchfinder or inquisitor.

Those with the coin or the right connections have more opportunity than most. The colleges and former University of Magic, have offered such individuals a scholarly route to understanding their powers and using them for the greater good – whether that is in the army as a battle mage, a geomancer in the Masons' Guild, or runecrafting armaments for the knights and soldiers on the front lines. And here, clearly lies a contradiction – as magic has been proven to make a positive contribution to society, most notably in the defence of the realm against insidious threats such as the Legion of Shadow.

These privileged few are, however, the exception. The average commoner does not have such avenues with which to pursue their art and gain mastery over it. Wild mages may number in their hundreds throughout the kingdom, of varying strength and ability. Without any protection from the four walls of a college or other approved institution, they remain pariahs that can be shunned by Valeron society at large and even hunted down by the Church.

In the last fifty years or so, there has been mounting rumours of a secret organisation known simply as the Arcane Hand. Those that seek out its agents may find protection and even guidance on how to use their powers. It's an organisation more secretive than the Thieves' Guild and for good reason – as the Church is actively seeking out leads to find its leaders and uproot its secret cells of operation, which appear to have influence in most of the major settlements around Valeron.

The ultimate aim of the Hand is unknown, although there have been whispers that it has links with the archmage Belshazzar, the vizier of the Khitesh city of Quadis. He has always had a reputation as a maverick, his city having long been a hub of esoteric learning. Mages flock to its infamous souk and bazaars, seeking magical artefacts, demon khas, and tomes of dark sorcery. Known to be ambitious and shrewd, it would come as no surprise to anyone if such a man was pulling the strings of this organisation.

Those that get recruited by the Arcane Hand often find themselves on errands and quests to satisfy some higher goal – one that will often remain intentionally hidden from the agents. It appears that the organisation imparts only fragments of information to each individual, so that the bigger picture is made impossible to piece together. Whether their ultimate purpose is nefarious in nature or not, it is undeniable that this organisation is helping to give refuge to many mages who face persecution and even death.

The Church
For some, the Church is a comfort and refuge – offering people a faith in a benevolent entity that cares for every mortal life on Dormus. Judah's teachings have always had a profound influence within Valeron society – each city, town and village having at least one place of worship. Their many steeples and spires serve as a constant reminder of the Church's presence. Comfort for some, but not for everyone.

The Church is opposed to magic and the Shroud. Judah spoke of such evils many times, as did the angels during their missionary tours. Magic is linked with demonism and as such, it represents an act of worship to Aisa – the Fate who is in opposition to the One God. Following such doctrine, the Church has always had a strict view of those who practice such arts – and has been responsible for many trials and executions of mages, and the burning of esoteric texts they deem apostasy. With the creation of the magic colleges and university, the Church was somewhat neutered – although, these institutions have always served the wealthy and well-connected. Those outside such circles are left to fend for themselves. These so-called wild mages are seen as a danger by the Church and their most dedicated servants have no qualms in capturing and removing such threats from society.

The Church has waxed and waned in power over the centuries, but now it appears to be rising again due to recent events. The appointment of Cardinal Rile as regent has meant that the Church has a spokesperson sitting in the highest position of power in the kingdom. The current dissolution of the Council of Nine has further bolstered the Cardinal's supremacy – with the royal palace in Assay now becoming a fortress guarded by templars and inquisitors. A new and tyrannical oppression is already starting to be felt, as inquisitors join and lead the city watches to help dispense justice. Newly commissioned witchfinders ride out across the realm, their keen eyes and instincts trained to root out wild magics and dark practices. The populace, who have enjoyed significant freedoms in past years, are now wary and suspicious – for everyone has some guilt to hide, and none can truly tell which of their sins might draw the ire of the Church.

Enclaves of the Wild

In order to heal her world, Kismet channelled her magic across Dormus, laying out a pattern of leylines that would help spread her life-giving energies. These powerful conduits helped give rise to the verdant forests, jungles and wildlife of Dormus, and continue to pulse with those same energies today.

Wood elementals from the Shroud were drawn to Dormus by these energies, particularly where leylines cross forming powerful nodes of vigorous life force. These elementals manifested themselves as the elder trees, pushing their deep roots into the earth to tap into the nourishing leyline energies. Although born from the Shroud, these elementals remain benign creatures, seeking to nurture and protect nature in all of its forms.

As threats to the wild places have increased throughout the ages, whether from roving bands of corrupted creatures or humanity's expansion, the elder trees have invariably needed guardians to help defend their groves. Those that have heeded this call are invited to drink of the sacred sap of the elder tree. This creates a covenant that will dedicate that individual's life to the protection of the grove. In return, the individual is able to tap into the leyline energies and use these to craft powerful spells and enchantments.

The females that take of the sap become dryads. Amongst their many gifts, they are given the ability to command animals – often taking these as pets, such as the hawk-like talon wings that are skilled scouts and hunters. They also have night vision and the ability to navigate the tangled wilds of their habitat with ease. However, if they stray too far from the source of their elder tree, then they can steadily wilt and die – so they must always maintain a close proximity to their grove.

Physically, the dryads retain their human features, but often manifest other characteristics, such as a green, brown or orange hue to their skin and hair, and an amber glow to the eyes. Their vigorous magics can also

extend their lifespans, with some dryads living many hundreds of years. The oldest dryad is always the leader of the grove – known as a dryad queen. On their passing, the next eldest dryad automatically becomes queen and takes over rulership of the grove.

Males can also partake of the sap, although their reactions to it can be more extreme and transformative. Whilst they do not suffer the same restrictions of distance as the dryads and can be away from the grove for many weeks without effect, their bodies will often undergo considerable change, replacing their humanity with something more bestial. These servants, known as satyrs, usually manifest bark-like skin, horns, and even fur on their bodies. A rare few might even become thornlocks, creatures that are more tree than man, and able to command wood elementals from the Shroud. Sadly, most end up losing their humanity entirely – becoming either creatures of the woods or tree-like guardians, rooted forever in the earth of their groves.

The dryads and their male-kin seek to protect their elder tree at all costs. Inevitably, this has brought them into conflict with others who would seek to harm the forests and wild places of Dormus. The leylines play a crucial role in helping to cleanse the world of the Shroud's encroaching corruption. Should the elder trees fall, then the crossroads of leylines can easily become infected by more malign spirits, and that can cause corruption to spread quickly and powerfully throughout the land.

Because of their singular dedication to protecting a grove, these guardians have little interest in the affairs of the world outside their borders – however, occasionally, they will offer aid to those they deem worthy of their respect. They have often provided a safe haven for the Wiccan in times of need and have even instructed them in the ways of nature magic. Some individuals also dedicate themselves to the protection of a grove, but choose not to take of the sap – so that they can operate within the wider world in a way that the dryads and satyrs cannot. These rangers often have many powers gifted them by their grove, making them perfect guides and protectors for others who may need to traverse the wilds.

The Halli

The people of the Saskat Prairies have much in common with the Wiccan, suggesting a shared ancestry – but at some point, certain tribes clearly deviated and chose to venture south into the vast grasslands, developing their own separate culture and traditions.

Known commonly as 'the horse people', the Halli live in nomadic tribes that range across the extensive savannah plains. They typically follow the seasonal migration paths of the bison and mastodons, which move north in the hot summer months and then return southwards in winter. These beasts provide the Halli with most of their resources, such as meat, bone, leather and fur.

Their nickname derives from their ability to tame and ride the highly-prized akala horses that roam the plains. These dun-coloured steeds are considered the fastest horses on Dormus, with incredible endurance to outlast most other breeds. The Halli are also expert at using bows and slings from horseback – exhibiting a skill that even exceeds the best of the Mordland cavalry.

As a people, they have only one permanent settlement known as Nawa. Set around several large lakes, this bustling town is also home to other settlers and pioneers – such as traders, hunters and explorers. However, the town is divided into two districts, with the inner section closed to those of non-Halli blood. The reason for this is that Nawa was built as a means for the Halli to protect their burial grounds, which are set around the slopes of the mountain rivers. These lands are considered sacred and any non-Halli setting foot on these would be killed on sight. One tribe is chosen every five years to settle in Nawa and be its guardians. After those five years have expired, another tribe replaces them, and so the cycle continues. Once a year, tribes will converge on Nawa to pay their respects. Rather than this being a solemn occasion, there is much feasting and celebration – and many travellers from around Dormus are drawn to Nawa for this reason, to partake of the festivities and also trade with the various tribes.

Like their Wiccan brothers, the Halli warriors will tattoo their bodies with colourful patterns. However, for the Halli these are purely decorative and are to mark various achievements and milestones in their lives. As a society, the Halli tend to distrust magic and stay away from anything with links to the arcane. However, the one exception to this is their shamans – of which there are usually two or three in each tribe. These are well versed in alchemy and magic, and have learned – through the ages – how to craft their own dreamcatcher staffs. These

extraordinary weapons are believed to combine the threads of crystal spiders with the feathers of a phoenix. Runes then feed magic through the circular arrangement, which the shaman can use to channel magic and even spirit animals from the Norr. The Halli pay their shamans great respect, for the outcome of many a hunt or a battle has been made victorious by the intervention of their magics.

In its arrogance, Valeron has laid claim to the prairie lands and made some efforts to settle around its periphery. But, because of the vast size of these imposing barrens, scouts and raiding parties have been unable to adequately penetrate its interior. The endless grasslands and maze-like canyons pose a formidable environment, riddled with deadly predators and poisonous vegetation, as well as debilitating temperatures in the heights of the summer months. Apart from some rare alchemic resources, Valeron has found no significant worth in the region, and therefore has not sort to plunder it or conquer its peoples.

The Halli are well adapted to survival in the prairies – and have therefore largely avoided the genocide that has plagued their Wiccan cousins. Therefore, as a people, they are flourishing, with new tribes constantly emerging and spreading out across the expansive plains to stake their own territories. Occasionally, some Halli do become lured by the tales of adventure brought to them by travellers and traders, and decide to seek a new life in the east. Often, these individuals, on account of their skilled horsemanship and survival skills, find themselves snapped up by mercenary companies or even the king's army. And there is a saying that, when a Halli gives his word and his weapon – it is for life.

The Noble Families

The wealthiest families in Valeron can trace their lineage back to the early days of Valeron's history, often drawing some ancestral link to a great king or influential leader. Over time, such families have accumulated great fortunes, often laying claim to vast estates and holdings throughout Valeron. Their greed for power and status both inside and outside of court, has led to many bitter rivalries. Scheming and backstabbing are the order of the day, with constant feuds and precarious bargaining leading to an ever-shifting landscape of loyalties and betrayals.

The heads of each noble house are known as dukes and duchesses. Some of these act as elected governors in the cities around Valeron or have responsibilities to garrison key areas of the kingdom. Each house will have its own regiments of loyal knights, who are sworn to serve both their house and their king. In times of war, such knights are expected to serve in the army alongside the regular soldiers. These campaigns can often make or break the political standing of a noble house, should their knights prove valorous or – by contrast – incur the shame of defeat. Those that laude praises on their patron family can expect great wealth and status for themselves, earning the title lord or lady.

The eldest son of each family is known as a count and carries most of the social and political responsibilities of their house. Other sons and daughters are given the title baron or baroness. Even within families, there can be competition and political manoeuvring. It is not unknown for barons to recruit spies, assassins and mercenary companies, to both protect their interests and to aid them in uncovering the secrets and plans of others. Paranoia and mistrust can be rife – and more than a few masquerade balls and grand parties can end their proceedings with sharp words and sharper blades.

For the most part, the noble families lead a decadent lifestyle, as befits those who can operate above the law. With ample coin at their fingertips, all the vices of the world are theirs for the taking – from illicit drugs and spices, to lavish and debauched revelries where all pleasures can be sated. Rumours and scandal often hint at darker inclinations amongst the elite. Some believe that many of the oldest and most influential families are infected with vampirism – others speak of demon worship and vile sorceries, and infernal pacts that span many centuries.

The nobles scheme and play within their own social world, almost entirely detached from the rest of reality. They look down contemptuously on the commonfolk, seeing them as merely fodder, with no real use other than to further their own games and schemes. To them, these commoners make up the 'vulgar masses', which can be toyed with and manipulated at will. Yet, occasional charitable acts and donations are not unheard of, should a family seek to boost their reputation and garner popular support. But such acts are done for selfish reasons and political manoeuvring, rather than altruism. The nobles will always act for themselves, seeking to exert their dominance over others and maintain their standing at the head of the social pyramid.

The Shadowborn

Aisa gifted the world of Umbril to one of her most loyal demon servants, Shimaza. The human populace of this shadow world had already turned to demon worship and were experimenting with rune magic, using what they had learned from the titans to further their own machinations. They had been looking for a way to fight back against the powerful creatures of darkness that stalked their world – a realm that had little light, save for a pale disc that passed for a sun. When they summoned the demons, these powerful beings initially acted as servants to the humans, helping them in their plight and gaining their trust. That was a mistake. As more of their twisted brethren came through into the world, ripping open tears in the fabric of the mortal plane, an invasion had begun. Those who chose to fight were swiftly killed, however there were many that saw the power that these beings wielded and willingly surrendered. These became the Nevarin – in the infernal language of demons, the word means 'slave'.

These Nevarin were marked by their overlord, Shimaza: three glowing serpents of runic magic, typically branded on an arm or across a chest. This shadow mark would bestow extraordinary powers on their bearer, channelled from the great demon himself. The Nevarin were to join the ranks of the Legion of Shadow, becoming eternal servants of Shimaza, bound to his will.

With the opening of the shadow gate, Shimaza's demonic legion was able to invade Dormus, with the aim of bringing it to ruin. However, they were not prepared for the valiant defence of Valeron by its people, who exhibited a brave and robust spirit that had been sorely lacking in those that had fallen on Umbril. The legion was defeated, however not all of its agents – both Nevarin and demon – fell during that war. Instead, knowing that defeat was now inevitable, they fled into the mountains and dark places of the world, where they could regroup and plan revenge.

Due to the magic that pumps through their shadow mark, the Nevarin are immortal. Therefore, they have been able to hatch plans that have spanned many centuries. Not only that, but the brand gives them a shared consciousness – in effect, they are not individuals but part of a symbiotic hive mind that connects each Nevarin with their master, Shimaza. This connectedness allows them to shapeshift, taking on the body of any other Nevarin who is linked to the faction by their brand. Similarly, on death they do not pass back to the weave. Their essence, infused with shadow magic, becomes a wisp that can craft a new body over time. Sometimes, this can take hours for one who is powerful in the ways of such arts, whilst for others it can take days or even weeks to manifest a new body. This means that even death is no obstacle to these powerful agents, who continue to serve their master on Dormus and conspire to bring this final world to ruin.

The Thieves' Guild

Whilst never formerly recognised by the Council of Nine in Assay, the Thieves' Guild has always exerted its influence on the dealings of Valeron society and the wider world. Some say that nothing happens without the knowledge of the Guild, who are expert at uncovering secrets and moving information. With contacts within the Merchants' Guild and the City Watch, this secretive organisation sits at the centre of a vast web of intrigue, manipulating events from the shadows.

Many may associate the Guild with acts of burglary, pickpocketing and illegal brawls, but such daily crimes are the domain of street gangs and petty crime lords – and not the Guild. Instead, the agents within its organisation specialise in more astute endeavours, such as forgery, assassination, spying and blackmail. These are the ways that people are bought and battles are won.

Most of the city gangs are orphans and homeless vagrants, looking for some chance of survival on the mean streets. They'll often take on the lowly jobs given to them by their crime lord or gang boss, as a means of getting recognised. Every street urchin and robber aspire to be accepted into the Guild proper. Usually this is through recommendation or by reputation. To enter the Guild is a privilege, for its agents will always look after their own – having a fierce loyalty for one another that is often lacking in more legitimate organisations. Nevertheless, there is a pecking order, and new recruits must work their way up the ladder, steadily unveiling more of the secrets of the Guild with each step.

No one knows for sure who is the head of the Guild, for it has many so-called leaders – each one likely to have a multitude of aliases and disguises. Few ever get to meet these infamous rogues, often only receiving their direction through other contacts or sources. This has

given these individuals a level of almost legendary status. Names such as Silent Whitt, Elyssa the Spider, Burns Ramsay, and The Phantom, can strike fear in the hearts of any urban dweller – for some say that these powerful individuals have eyes and ears everywhere, and woe to those who foolishly find themselves drawing their ire.

The Travellers (Siun Danai)
The colourful painted wagons of the travelling people were once a common sight in Valeron, their storytellers and bards welcomed as a prized source of news and rumours from throughout the land. Villagers and townsfolk would see their arrival as a prelude to a time of celebration and carnival, when the gaudy tents would rise like a forest around the settlement, promising exotic wonders and indulgences that only the travellers could provide.

Entertainers would take to the streets, performing sleight-of-hand tricks or acrobatic performances that would draw gasps of amazement. Within the tents, where incense smoke curls and coalesces, fortunes would be read from the cards or visions seen within clouded crystals. Adults would dance around the fires to the fiddle and the flute, while their children sat entranced by the boisterous puppet plays – recounting grand adventures or giving sage advice. Then the traders would come, hawking their wares. Some trinkets and potions for luck or love, a wooden charm for the fields to bring the rain. Perhaps a remedy for a cold or that incessant cough, or maybe a cream to restore one's lost youth. Like colourful rains, the travellers would descend, bringing light and joy and music. Then just like a brief summer shower, they would be gone again – leaving nothing in their wake but memories and wonder.

Such a story might be one they themselves would spin, but the reality has been very different – certainly in the last few hundred years as society has become ever more guarded and suspicious of outsiders. The travellers have been a people that have forever lived outside the rules and laws of others, refusing to bow to any ruler – or observe any boundary or border. In former times, they were a crucial supply of news and gossip from both near and far, helping communities to stay connected with the wider world – one that was often wild and dangerous, and best not travelled lightly. Overtime, better maintained roads and the presence of wardens, has meant travel has become more commonplace, with cities, towns and villages safer to journey between. News can now travel fast, by merchants, messengers and adventurers – meaning that the travellers are no longer such an essential resource.

Their carnivals were once a welcome sight, offering a multitude of diversions to escape the mundanity of everyday life. But the influence of the Church has shifted people's perceptions of such pastimes – particularly as the travellers have garnered a reputation for witchcraft, deceit and thievery. Few settlements are now keen to see the arrival of the coloured wagons – and it can be a relief to see them on the move again. Those that do succumb to their charms however, often end up benefiting from the news and goods that the travellers have to share, and the colourful entertainments that can offer a much-needed tonic if times are hard.

Pushed frequently to the margins of society, the travellers are now dwindling in number and their long traditions mostly fading into memory. However, there are still some bands traversing the wilds, usually consisting of several extended families. They still practice some of their arts, mostly of performance and chicanery, but there are those amongst the families that do have a real affinity for magic – particularly that of mind magic, perhaps suggesting links with the Khiteshi nomads. Their skills in woodcraft and trinket-making can be highly sought after, and their wares will often fetch good prices in the markets around Valeron. Whilst few of their charms probably have the powers to which they claim, there has been more than one unsuspecting customer getting more than they bargained for.

Despite their changing fortunes, travellers are a happy and hospitable people, and can often be a source of relief for other travellers and adventurers seeking company out on the roads. Travellers are always happy to share their fires and their stories with others – and for those that accept such an invitation, they might leave with rare knowledge, valuable rumours and even strange wares from the distant reaches of the land.

The Wiccan

During the Dark Ages, the tribes of man started to build permanent settlements and unite under great leaders known as kings. Such loyalty brought some protection, but also meant that those sworn to

a ruler would be bound to fight for their overlord. Whilst many found the permanence of a home and land a fair pay off for such a service, there were others that preferred to cling to their own freedoms and independence – and not be beholden to tyrannical leaders and their shifting rivalries.

These outsiders would come to call themselves the Wiccan, a Dark Age word that was often used in a derogatory fashion to label them ('witch people') but one they have gladly accepted and owned. Indeed, they have always had an affinity for magic since the time of the dwarves, who willingly shared their knowledge during the wars with the Dours. Many of their people openly practice such magics and have fused them with knowledge from the dryad enclaves, to form their own variations of runic and druidic magic. The Wiccan warriors will paint or tattoo their bodies with sigils of power, which bestow upon them great strength and physical endurance. Their mages can often reach into the Shroud, pulling lesser demons and elementals into the physical plane to serve as minions – and a rare few have even mastered the powers of shapeshifting, taking on the forms of spirit animals such as wolves and bears.

Over time, the Wiccan were pushed further westwards by the expansion of kingdoms such as Amaral and Valeron, until they found themselves in the marshy fenlands of a region they named Gilglaiden – 'Land of Hope'. At first, it lived up to its promise. The Wiccan were able to beat back many of the goblins, gnolls and other tribes that infested the land, and started to carve out some semblance of a home. Some clans made permanent settlements, often situated next to barrows where they would bury and honour their dead heroes. Others, chose to remain nomadic, and would travel the land, always desiring to discover new regions and make fresh discoveries.

This hopeful start was not to last. With the coming of Saint Allam and the armies of the Church, the Wiccan suddenly found their lands under threat. Despite Allam's attempts to garner peace and safe passage, it was quickly clear to the Wiccan that these interlopers were here to seek land and resources at whatever the cost – acting on the orders of a desperate king.

War was inevitable. Wiccan settlements were torched and their age-old treasures pillaged for the king's treasury. Those that did fight back found themselves outmatched by the heavy armour and divine magics of the knights and inquisitors. The Wiccan that surrendered fared little better, for often families were divided and some taken prisoner to ensure loyalty. Others were expected to join the crusade and turn their weapons against their own kinsfolk.

Gilglaiden was eventually claimed by the king and settled by the people of Valeron. The Wiccan were forced to scurry away like rats, to cling to the forests and mountains that offered sanctuary. They were few in number now and hadn't the strength to take back what had once been theirs.

In the last few years, a spirit of rebellion has sparked within these remaining Wiccan. A great hero and chieftain, known as Conall, has united tribes under his banner. Although their forces are limited, they are driven by a desire for revenge – and to see Valeron pay for the crimes it has committed. Against the odds, Conall sacked the walled town of Carvel, which had become a thriving centre of pilgrim worship. During the fighting, he also took the life of the king's middle son, Lazlo. Conall's victory was enough to lure other tribes to his side, including the Wolfpaw and Moonshade clans. Now, Conall intends to continue his advance eastwards into the Heartlands, to sate his anger and to see Valeron burn.

7
Heroes (and Villains) of Valeron

The celestial weave hangs across the heavens, each of its strands given the power of destiny by the sacrifice of Gabriel. When Aisa rebelled against the cosmic plan, she introduced chaos to the weave, unravelling that grand vision and setting it on a different course. Gabriel gave his life to try and correct its path. With his passing, each individual in the weave was gifted a greater role to play in spinning its future – for better or for ill.

Some threads of the weave shine brighter than others, infused with the power to influence its pattern. These are the great men and women of fame, heroes (or villains) who command the web of destiny and can spin its threads anew, changing lives and history, influencing kings and nations, and furthering the causes they believe are right. Some may not even consider themselves special or significant, and yet even the smallest decision or hard-won victory can create the ripples that soon become the waves of change.

For those threads that shine less bright, there is still a role to play in this grand plan – each life spanning a myriad of choices and consequences. And even these might raise up great legends or lay claim to fabulous achievements, becoming part of the great story that is forever being spun.

Important note: Some biographies contain major plot spoilers for the first three books in the DestinyQuest saga – *The Legion of Shadow*, *The Heart of Fire* and *The Eye of Winter's Fury*.

Arran Vallimere – the Ghost Prince

The third son of King Leonidas was born prematurely, his mother losing her life during the long and painful birth. He was weak and sickly, and not expected to live past the week. His father had little care for his son's fate, too grief stricken at the loss of his beloved wife to ever look upon the child. Against the odds, Arran did survive and grew to be a young man, although he would always remain a frail and brooding individual, perpetually tormented by nightmarish dreams. Around the palace they called him the ghost prince, because he preferred to stay out of sight, never wanting to draw attention unlike his extroverted brothers. More often than not, he would be found in the library, poring over stories of adventure and imagining himself the bold knight that saved the day.

As Leonidas grew increasingly ill, afflicted with some wasting malady, Cardinal Rile started to exercise his authority within the palace. The Wiccan threat was a cause for concern and gave Rile his excuse to remove Arran from the city – one less royal in the way of his bid for power. And so, Arran was given an assignment: to lead a retinue of knights and palace guard to the castle of Lord Salton, to help bolster the garrison's defences and slow the Wiccan advance. Arran was naturally confused by such an errand, but Rile convinced him that a royal leading the troops would be a boon for morale. Arran accepted, swayed by the idea that he might finally be living out one of the many adventures he had read about in his storybooks.

The reality of life on the road proved him wrong. After weeks of gruelling travel, it became apparent that something was wrong. He sensed it in the nervousness of the knights and the grim demeanour of the inquisitor who accompanied him. Rile had brought him out here for a reason – and it wasn't to play the hero and defend the kingdom. While travelling through the bleak and rain-sodden hills north of Fernfall, the betrayal was revealed. Arran and the palace guards had been brought here to their deaths – and the inquisitor and his knights were the executioners. Before they could act, however, the group was attacked by a raiding party of Wiccan. In the chaos of the fight, Arran escaped into the hills. He ran blindly into the lashing rain, not knowing where he might find safety. His panicked flight would eventually lead him into the forested highlands, where he fell victim to a ferocious pack of wolves.

Too weak and exhausted to defend himself, Arran stared down the alpha leader, a giant grey-haired predator that he had no hope of defeating. There was only one outcome. But destiny was to play its hand. As the wolf leapt forward, Arran felt a force push into his body – a bear spirit from the Norr that suddenly emboldened him with strength. Miraculously, he was able to fight back and defeat the wolf. But the wounds he sustained were too much. Lost and alone, he stumbled through the cold and unforgiving wilderness until his strength finally gave out. He was found a day later by a trapper, who brought Arran to the nearby citadel of Bitter Keep. Lord Everard, the garrison commander, recognised the boy immediately as Prince Arran. His attendants did all they could to save the boy, but the outlook was bleak – and made worse by the news that Leonidas and his eldest son, Malden, had been murdered in the capital. Arran was the last surviving heir to the throne.

Once again, despite the odds, Arran miraculously survived. But his experience would leave him forever changed. His body had been ravaged by the wounds he had sustained and the frostbite from his exposure to the elements. By all accounts, he should have been dead. But there was a power inside of him that was sustaining his life, even though his physical body was essentially a corpse. Somehow, the bear spirit that he had encountered in the wild was feeding him strength. The weak and sickly boy had become transformed – his body now a hulking mass of hardened muscle and sinew. In death he had been given a new life, a new start.

Bitter Keep was destroyed by a terrible earthquake that ripped across the northern reaches. Arran was one of the few survivors. Finding himself alone once again, he trekked north into the frozen wilds of Skardland,

now cut off from the south by the seismic upheaval. Impervious to the bitter cold, Arran was able to survive in his newfound environment. His wayward journey finally brought him to a Skard encampment. After proving his strength to them, he gained their loyalty. In him they saw a chance to free the soul of their missing leader, Skoll Frostgrieve. Arran learnt how to project his spirit into the Norr and with the help of his bear companion, he was able to free Skoll from his entrapment. He learnt that a witch was behind the tremors that were plaguing the land. She was trying to release an age-old demon known as Jormungdar.

Skoll and Arran ranged north, passing through the imposing mountain range known as the North Face, and emerging in the magic-ravaged lands beyond. Here, they finally met the witch known as Melusine – a former Mordland princess who had once been imprisoned for the murder of a Valeron king. She had been plotting her revenge ever since. Arran defeated the witch, but her plan had already come to fruition. The great demon was released, a gargantuan monstrosity that had the power to end the world. Luckily, the beast was not at full strength. With the help of a Skard army, now united for the first time in many years, Arran was able to defeat the demon. Skoll sustained a fatal wound during the battle. Before he gave his last breath, he passed command of the Skards to Arran, who was now to lead them as their new Drokke.

Arran had cast away his corpse-body, his heightened powers now enabling him to exist as a spirit – a ghost. He had become, in essence, what those in the palace had always deemed him. A ghost prince. But now he wanted revenge. He wanted the throne that was rightfully his. The lands of the north were riven with crevices and rifts from Jormungdar's release. The journey south would not be easy, but Arran believed there had to be a way through the underworld, dangerous though that may be. The Skards swore their allegiance to their new Drokke – and together they prepared to make the perilous journey into the underworld and help Arran win his crown. Their fate remains unknown.

Avian Dale – the Fallen Archon

It was barely dawn as the grey-robed figure walked the quiet streets of Lull, a chill fog obscuring much of the surroundings. The year was 479 of the Ascendant. King Wynne had sat the throne for over a decade. In that time, he had already promised much for those on the margins of society – the persecuted and the forgotten. There was even talk of a university being built in Talanost, to train mages in the fickle arts of the arcane. These were strange times indeed, where tolerance for the eccentric and macabre was becoming more accepted. Perhaps the sanatorium was a product of that mindset. It loomed out of the mist, a tall pale stone building with a profusion of unnecessary spires in the old Frankish tradition. Arches yawned over the entrance to a cobbled courtyard where a fountain trickled its waters languidly, as if still waking up – like the rest of the populace.

The stranger met with the clerk, a small gaunt woman with spectacles perched on the end of her nose. He explained his business in a smooth but commanding tone. He was here to visit a patient, whose name was Avian Dale. The clerk blinked back surprise, then scratched her head. Taking a set of keys, she led the stranger down a darkened hall. Each footstep was accompanied by screams and sobbing. Somewhere, a door was being rattled – sounding like it might be ripped from its hinges. A gargling cry. Someone singing, a sad mournful melody. As the stranger made his way past the iron doors, set into crumbling stonework, he heard every sad tale of insanity and madness. Finally, they ascended a small winding staircase to another floor, identical to the last. Here, the screams were louder – unending. The grey-robed man didn't flinch or show concern. His expression was hidden beneath the darkness of his cowl.

They came to a door. The clerk gave a heavy sigh, then started to thumb through the many iron keys. She selected one then placed it in the door. A rattle and then a click. Quickly, she scuttled backwards, as if whatever was inside made her afraid. 'Half an hour', she said warningly. Then she scarpered away, much like the rats that plagued the streets. The stranger pulled back his hood. A thin and narrow face, pale as the morning mist. Unremarkable and forgettable, even his eyes seemed to lack any vibrancy of life. He pushed on the door with spidery fingers. A creak as it opened, revealing the cramped and austere cell. Just a pallet bed and a bucket, and a tiny crack of light seeping through an afterthought of a window. It was barely enough to illuminate the man lying on the bed, his wrists shackled in irons. He was curled up, rocking back and forth, quietly sobbing. He was meant to be young, maybe no older than seventeen summers, but he was clearly malnourished – his

face like a skull, dark hollows for the eyes. His blotched and bruised skin was stretched tight over the bones. He could have passed for a fresh corpse.

The grey-robed man knelt beside the sobbing Avian Dale, his head tilted as if trying to take the measure of this wrecked life that lay before him. When he spoke, it was with soft words, almost a whisper, but they commanded attention. He said his name was Uzahl Epius – and he was going to give Avian a new life. The young patient's eyes widened, a gasping wheeze escaping his broken lips. This wretched creature had never been afforded hope before – not for many years. Uzahl nodded. He placed a hand on the chains and with a blurring of grey light, both manacles shattered in two. He then proceeded to lift the man into his arms with a strength belying his slender physique – although there wasn't much of Avian save for skin and bone. There was a brief moment as the stranger closed his eyes, taking a deep breath as if to compose himself. Then a flicker of grey light, and they were gone. Only scuffed boot prints in the dust and a pair of broken manacles to suggest they had ever been there.

Avian Dale had been marked for greatness, a child prodigy that seemed blessed by the One God. His parents had both been acolytes in the congregation at Lull and had raised Avian in the truth of the scriptures. Even from a young age, he exercised a startling command of the divine light, able to heal the sick with the skill that a trained medic would take years to achieve. For sure, he was almost destined to become a white abbot and his reputation, even as a young boy, was spreading far and wide. However, at the age of seven, Avian started to have dreams and visions. At first, these were sporadic and fluctuated between lucid and serene visions of a holy nature to horrific nightmares that would leave him shivering and sobbing. While this raised concern, it only served to denote how special this boy really was. His parents were sure that his condition would pass and perhaps it was a product of his powerful inner kha, that needed more maturity to be mastered and controlled.

Sadly, the visions only got worse – until Avian would be lost for days, either in some joyful delirium or a nightmare that he could not awaken from. In the few hours that he would awake and gain control of his senses, he would be unable to speak of what he had witnessed.

Instead, he would beg for death. To not have to endure this life any longer. His parents invited many to try and heal their son and even resorted to some pagan tonics when all else failed. But nothing could break the cycle of their son's decline. In the end, he was assigned to the sanatorium – with the expectation that he would be dead by the age of twelve. Somehow, he had defied those odds. Perhaps his kha was keeping him alive somehow, for he was barely eating or drinking. The years drifted by, but the boy's malady only worsened – the nightmares more frequent. In the end, his parents stopped their visits. They simply accepted that their beloved son was lost. Death would be a mercy, but their faith could not condone such an act.

Uzahl placed Avian within the circle of runes, marked out in a dizzying array of spirals and sigils. Then he walked its perimeter, checking there were no breaks in the arcane script, no mistakes that would ruin the spell. Then he motioned with his hand, a grey ripple of magic spreading out from his fingertips and flowing into one of the runes, making it shine brighter than before, illuminating the stonework of the tower with a crimson glow. Avian was struggling to rise, fearful of what he was witnessing. He tried to speak, but his voice was just a hoarse croak. Uzahl showed no concern, instead he stepped around the circle and proceeded to ignite another rune. With a flush of colour, magic swept around the circle and engulfed the young man at its centre in coruscating light. A bright flash, a smell of brimstone. Avian threw back his head, body convulsing. From his mouth, a white tendril of mist snaked out to coalesce in a cloud about the circle, then another flash and the mist was gone. The young man flopped back lifeless on the cold dark stones.

Avian's eyes flashed open. He stood beneath a vast storm-wracked sky, its broiling clouds lit by a sickly green radiance. All around him, a blackened wasteland that stretched towards an infinite horizon, broken only by the twisted spires of black rock that raked at the sky. He looked down at himself, dressed in the same ragged sanatorium robe, body as thin and broken as it had been before. He was trapped in another vision, another nightmare. But this felt more real – more alive. Then the landscape seemed to shift and blur. He had the sensation of movement, a sickening lurch. He couldn't tell if he was travelling somehow or the world around him was moving and shifting beneath his feet. Unable to maintain his balance, he stumbled and fell. When he hit the ground, his palms slapped against smooth stone. Looking up, he saw he was in a courtyard of some ruined castle or fortress. Unlike the rest of this hellish landscape, it was illuminated in a bright golden light – and that light was coming from a shining and radiant being. It was taller than a man, with wings that stretched back from its shoulders, bright as twin suns. Avian raised a hand to shade his eyes, squinting into the golden brilliance.

The archon was a demon of light. When it spoke, its words were like music – a cascade of notes that reverberated in the stillness of that gloomy place. By some miracle, Avian found that he could understand the language, the melodies turning to words in his mind. The archon told him everything. When Judah died, his essence went back to Kismet to be reborn. Time shifts differently in the heavens and the physical plane. Avian was the reborn Judah, given his powerful essence that had once changed a world – a bright and shining thread that streaked out across the weave. But Kismet's corruption had tainted the power of that pure born. Avian was the product. A corrupted messiah, whose mind now touched that of the great Yu'Weh, and was cursed to share his eternal dreams and nightmares, the joys and horrors only a god should have known. For a mortal it would be a madness without end.

But Avian still had Judah's power in his body, within the fibres of his being. An inner kha that was powerful and fully formed. And the archon wanted it for himself. It would be the perfect fusion of demon magic and divine light, the equilibrium that the archon had been seeking for hundreds of years. He had tried in vain to cultivate this twin power in his earthly followers, but even those that had some mastery – like the great Uzahl – could only maintain it for so long before one dominated the other, a constant warring of light and dark. To be a master of the grey took immense dedication and perhaps a little madness too.

Avian clearly had no choice in what was to occur. The archon simply gestured with a glowing hand and the young man's soul was thrown screaming into a jewelled prison of no escape. There he would remain bound, battering against walls that fractured his visage into a thousand agonised faces. A soul trapped in the Norr for eternity. On the physical plane, Uzahl had completed a further circle of runes around the lifeless corpse of Avian Dale. When he sparked their magic into life, the archon was summoned forth – and took possession of the former Avian Dale.

The young man's eyes flicked open, for a moment radiant with a golden light, then settling back to their original sky-blue hue. He rose, standing straight and proud, newfound strength pumping through a once weak and feeble body. Uzahl fell to his knees and praised his master, who had now been given life and body to perform the work that needed to be done.

The archon's magic made Avian immortal – and the fusion of the divine light within his body and the demon magic of the Shroud, gifted him extraordinary powers beyond what most archmages could achieve. At the University of Magic, he excelled as a student and then became a tutor. He was instrumental in aiding the mages that found and closed the Shadow Gate during the first invasion. Eventually, he would become an advisor to the king – many kings over the ages – and sit as primary speaker on the Council of Nine, with the title Grand Master of the Dawn.

During his vast and ageless lifetime, Avian has recruited many to his cause. These Grey Knights were handpicked for their prospective talents. Some were assassins and rogues, others former witchfinders or even templars, who may have fallen off the path – lost their way or purpose – and Avian had picked them up and breathed fresh life into them. He had a vision of what needed to be done. To create grey mages like himself, because he knew the grey magic had power over both the Shroud and the physical plane. It could heal rifts and tears in the fabric of reality, restoring the barrier between the two. As always, very few have proven any lasting mastery of the art for it takes practised discipline to maintain both a divine kha and the taint of the Shroud within a single body.

Avian Dale's last mission was to accompany one of his knights, a witchfinder known as Virgil Elland, into the haunted depths of a dwarven city known as Tartarus. An archdemon had uncovered the whereabouts of the ancient demon blade known as Ragnarok, that once wreaked havoc in ages past. Avian was determined to stop this demon from affecting the weave – and the fate of Dormus. However, after descending into the volcanic depths, Avian has not been heard from since. His Grey Knights have been left without leadership and fear the worst. If Avian Dale has fallen in battle, then a great hero has truly been lost – although, somewhere, deep in the shadowlands of the Norr, a young man still beats against the walls of his prison, tortured by his waking nightmares and visions. He can still feel his body on the physical plane, its heart pumping with the power of a divine messiah. Avian Dale's story may not yet be over. His thread still burns bright across the breadth of the heavens.

Baron Chester Fromark – the Mining Magnate

Father had brought his shame on the family name once again, which was really saying something considering how far they had all fallen. Chester was slouched on the chaise lounge, pouring himself a glass of wine from the crystal decanter, before the decanter was snatched away by the debt collectors. They'd been there for hours now, gradually stripping the home bare of all its belongings. He watched another enormous painting go out of the front doors. It was a fake, but guess that didn't matter much. When they started to move the chaise lounge, he finally had to lurch drunkenly to his feet, swaying as he eyed the coats slung across another collector's arms. They were his and he protested as much, but all he earned in response was the steely glare of the bruisers, armed with batons and blades. The muscle to make sure the debts were paid. Not that they were needed. Chester was in no state to fight back and, besides, he was an utter coward. Probably, ran like a streak through all the Fromarks.

Their fortunes had been on the wane for many generations, but Chester's father – Edgar Fromark– had really gone to town with driving their name into the dirt. He was a gambler and a drunk, something else that seemed to run strong in the family. His wife and Chester's mother left Edgar a good decade ago. And then Astrid Berglund came along to put a final nail in the coffin. She was a Skard, which was bad enough, but also a deadbeat mercenary. They had called her the Fortress, apparently on account of her height and strength, but Chester would argue she had a face like a wall and a smile like a broken portcullis. Somehow, she had fallen for the old Edgar Fromark. It didn't take a scholar to work out she was after the last of his money and he was a sucker for her attention. Their marriage was all rather scandalous. Chester didn't remember much; he was too drunk. But he did manage to recall that hardly any were in attendance, except those thoroughly desperate for gossip and to witness the ludicrousness of the match.

Since then, Chester had never seen either. They'd gone on their travels, which translated into Astrid dragging her new husband from city to city, seeing the sights but mostly the taverns, drinking them dry, then moving on – leaving debt and owed favours in their wake. Chester was now witnessing the aftermath. His family home in Greyspire was now as empty as his broken life. But ever the opportunist, Chester reacted by doing what he did best. Pulling up the floorboard in his room, he grabbed the last of his coin and gems, ferreted away for just such a day. Then he went and got drunk – very drunk. It seemed like the logical thing to do. In the taverns and gambling dens he knew what they called him. Baron Nomark. The good for nothing son of an equally good for nothing father. But his coin was still good, when he had it, and so he would snort spice and knock back the drinks, desperate for that modicum of peace to smooth off the rough edges of a life of disappointment.

The problem with coin is that, eventually it runs out. And when one is an idle layabout, it's not easily earned. Chester tried to call in some favours from friends, but learned he had none – at least, not any more. It seemed he owed everyone something and no-one wanted to give him a second chance. Even Chester's older brother, the count, refused his supplications – probably on account of his own waning fortunes and addictions. Chester was on his own. Then, to rub salt into the wound, he stumbled home one evening to find the place filled with squatters. He shrugged his shoulders. It felt rather fitting in an amusing way. So, he bedded down next to the nearest vagrant, although not before asking him if he had a coin to spare. He hadn't.

Sobriety was a scary state for Chester. It gave him opportunity to think and he really didn't like that. Desperate for his next drink, he wandered the cobbled streets looking for some small opportunity. He was even thinking of robbery. How hard could it be? He had a knife, albeit one that he'd only used to peel an apple or stake some meat. But perhaps he could use it in a menacing way. He practised some sneers in a shop window. He hadn't shaved or washed for a good few days – maybe longer. He certainly looked the part. The day was spent looking for his victim, but as the streets filled up with bustling crowds, it became almost impossible to find an opportunity. In the end, he slumped down on a doorstep, head in hands. Feeling hopeless and lost, he finally wondered if the knife might finally be put to a better use. That would

make another scandalous story for the royal courts. The Nomark found dead on the streets. Perhaps they wouldn't even know it was him.

It was then he heard the tinkle of something hitting the stone. He glanced up and saw the scattering of coins by his lap. Caught by surprise, he didn't think to look up to see who his mysterious benefactor had been. He reached out and snatched them with grubby hands, fearing that a moment's delay might see them disappear like some cruel enchantment. But they were real enough, cold and hard in his tight fists. It was only then that it occurred to him that someone had been responsible for this act of kindness. He looked around wildly, but the crowds gave him no answer – they hurried past, oblivious to his fate. But one of them had evidently taken pity on him. It suddenly made him feel sad to think that he had truly sunk so low, to need the charity of a stranger. It was a feeling that needed to be quashed as soon as possible. Chester pocketed his gains and set his gaze on the nearest gambling hall.

The coins were clearly charmed or perhaps Chester had reached rock bottom and was willing to do anything to redeem his failing fortune. He won his first couple of card games, which was rare enough. Sobriety had its uses. He could have bought a drink, a whole round of drinks in fact, but he realised for the first time that he could read people better when the room wasn't spinning or his head clouded with spice. Was this a talent he had been sourly missing all these years? He raked in the coin, forever raising the stakes. His opponents came and went, but all fell victim to Chester's newfound luck.

On his last game of the night, Chester was playing some grizzled old gentleman. He looked like he might have had a decent fortune once. His clothes had a fine cut and hinted at fashion, but the cuffs were wine-stained and the stitching of his jacket was coming loose. He was also drunk. Which Chester knew was to his advantage. He didn't need a knife to best someone, he could just use the cards. He bled the poor old soul dry. But the man wasn't giving up. He was desperate to win back what he had lost – but he had nothing else to stake. Chester had been there, knew the pain. At least he offered to buy the man a drink, which was gladly accepted. As the old gentleman supped on his ale, he reached into his jacket pocket and pulled out some papers. They were deeds to a mine in the west. Apparently, they'd brought him nothing but trouble and he wanted rid of them. He offered to swap, the money in the pot for those deeds.

Chester had won a fortune in coin and gems that night. It was enough to keep him in spice and wine for a month or two, at least. But he was staring at the deeds and found it hard to deny their lure. He had never owned anything before – at least nothing as grown-up and substantial as property. He quickly snatched the deeds from out of the man's hands and left there and then, so as not to second-think his decision or contemplate the coin he was giving away. He had just become the owner of a mine. Foolish and ridiculous, he would certainly agree, but maybe fortune really was smiling on him that day. As it turned out, it was. Chester Fromark had started his journey – from rags to riches.

The mine was a literal gold mine, as Chester was to discover. It had just been poorly managed. The miners were striking and understandably had no intention of returning to work. Apparently, a troll infestation in the lower caverns would do that – and the previous owner had no coin for mercenaries or adventurers to clear out the mine so work could continue. Chester didn't have the coin either but he did have an idea. He did something no mine owner in their right mind would ever do. He hired a local mercenary outfit – and instead of coin he gave them a stake in the mine. If it performed well and delivered, they'd profit just as he would. He never thought they'd bite but they took the bait. And they certainly kept up their side of the bargain, clearing out the mines and then guarding it from other threats. The miners returned to work and Chester stayed true to his word – the mercenaries got their cut of the profits. A tidy sum that was easy money for them.

Chester bought up the other ailing mines in the area. It was becoming clear that trolls were just the start of the problem. Much of these mountains were plagued with goblins, ogres and even cloud giants. Fromark hired more mercenaries, assembling an army of muscle that could clear out areas and then secure them. Such hired swords were ordinarily a fickle bunch, but with a stake in the mines, they remained loyal for the most part, and the miners benefitted from their presence. When word got out, other miners started to flock to Fromark's sites, desiring the security that was sadly lacking from the other mines, currently being run to ruin by the mining consortium.

Chester had made a name for himself. He bought homes in Assay and Solace, and enjoyed the finer things of life. He could have been content – and to an extent he was. He had achieved more than he ever thought he was capable of. But this was just the start. While at a party in the upper district of Solace, he met the retired opera singer Millie Genaro. She was nearly twenty years his senior, but he was captivated by her presence. She was dressed in the height of noble fashion at the time, a Frankish corset and flowing skirts, and a neck dripping with diamonds. She owned the room with her smile and her laughter, but there was a strength of presence there, a sharp and keen intelligence. Chester would say he had few talents, but one was certainly a charm with the ladies. The other nobles looked down on him as 'new money', an upstart that would soon land on his face. But Millie didn't treat him like that. She was self-made too and had earned a fortune on the opera circuit of the cities. The two hit it off immediately and eventually fell in love – a scandal once again, but at least for the right reasons. They were soon married, cementing a partnership that would soon bear many fruits.

Millie Genaro was a shrewd business woman. She had powerful contacts and a prominent stake in a number of businesses. With her substantial fortune as backing, Chester was able to make the mining consortium an offer they could not refuse – as it had become known to him that they were struggling to set up new operations and protect the ones they had. Fromark bought up most of the mines in western Valeron and hired prospectors to look for further opportunities in the mountain ranges of the south. With new industries starting to boom in the city of Kiln, where the forges always burned hot with activity, the buzz was now sparkpowder – and Fromark wanted a piece of that pie.

The Church and crown had monopolised its early developments, looking for a way to propel ballista bolts with greater force. The black powder proved incredibly volatile and difficult to produce in large quantities. The main reagent was a crystal known as seraphine – incredibly rare, it was discovered in small deposits in deep cave systems, often with bat populations as their guano appeared to galvanise the crystal formations. When dissolved in a solution and then heated, the resulting minerals could be extracted and combined with sulphur and charcoal to create sparkpowder. With Church funding, alchemists were able to refine their designs, finally developing the first flintlock mechanisms that added a triggering device to spark the powder and eject a missile. These flintlocks were first utilised in the field by witchfinders, who were keen to test them out against the creatures they hunted.

In alchemical circles, secrets rarely stay a secret. The chemical formula was inevitably leaked. Almost overnight, seraphine became the most desirable resource on Dormus. The Fromarks were quick to react to this sudden interest, funding research projects and searching out deposits of this rare commodity. Currently, its major centres are Venetia and Sargassi, who are dominating the trade – but Fromark is convinced the Terral Jungle to the south will be a treasure trove of seraphine. He is hiring explorers and speculators to explore the coastal caverns and venture deep into the tangled interior.

The Fromarks are considered one of the richest couples in the kingdom. Whilst the nobles may treat them as outsiders, there is certainly no mistaking their power and influence. The times are changing and new inventions and industry are increasingly set to influence the future. Most of the old money in Valeron is inherited and rarely earned – but the Fromarks are forging a bright future and paving the way for others with ingenuity and business savvy to grasp this new and exciting future with both hands.

Bern Farstrider – the Green Hood
Thornbrook Hall stood alone on the hill, a solitary and brooding presence fashioned from dark Perova stone. The storm had stolen the last of the fading sunlight and now black clouds broiled across the melancholy skies and spat a hissing rain that soon became a thunderous deluge, beating against the muddy earth. A warden walked the perimeter of the building, huddled in his coat, hat tugged low across his brow. Lantern light pooled around him but did little to penetrate the encroaching dark. Below, in the valley, distant pinpricks of light marked out the town of Whitechurch – a flickering constellation, visible for brief moments between the drifting banks of fog. The warden cast his eyes around one last time, his mind already made up to return to his quarters. There would be no trouble this night – even the beasts of the forest had more sense than to be out in this chill, lashing rain.

The crack of a twig. The warden swung round, hand moving to his blade. The dark was oppressive, made worse by the fog and thick curtains of rain. He walked forward a little way; lantern held aloft. But there was nothing. He snorted, realising that his nerves were most definitely getting the better of him this night. Then there was a flash of lightning – a staccato beat of bright whiteness. And standing there, only metres away was the silhouette of a man, rain drenched and shivering. The warden gave a cry, drawing his sword and demanding to know the stranger's intent. He watched as the man entered the pool of light. A young man, maybe in his early twenties – long hair plastered to his face. His leathers were black with the rain, a wool cloak sagging from his narrow shoulders. He said he was a traveller that had been set upon by wolves. His horse bolted – threw him off. Now, he had come begging for shelter.

The warden shooed him away, gesturing into the dark towards the town. The stranger continued to beg, raising his voice imploringly – showing that he was unarmed. The warden took an angry step forward. Things may have gone ugly, but then the door of the hall opened. A woman was standing there, framed in the light. She saw the poor, drenched young man and ushered him in – despite the grumbling from her warden. As the young man passed him, a deft move left a nick on the warden's arm. He would have barely felt it, but the sleep poison would soon do its work.

Inside, the young man was given food and fresh clothing. The woman was a countess of noble stock, newly married but alone this night save for her household of servants. After enjoying some warm stew prepared by the cook, the man – who called himself Oswald – was offered some blankets and a couch to sleep on. The countess retired to her quarters. At midnight, a clock chimed in some nearby room. The man sprang up, casting aside the blanket. Like a ghost, he moved quietly to the front door – silently pulling back the many bolts and chains. He pulled it open, ushering in the dark shadows from the rain. Four men, armed with an array of sacks – faces hidden with scarves. There was no fighting, no blood spilled. The countess slept soundly, while the thieves robbed her of her riches. Tapestries, gold, silver, ornaments – as much as they could safely carry. Then they bolted into the darkness. Back into the storm. They would be well on their way east by the time their crime had been

noticed, disappearing into the vast forested hills. There they would lie low, before heading to a local town — selling some of their wares and drinking the profits. These robbers had no need of the gold. They stole for the thrill and to drink and gamble. The nobles and other rich fools were just their playthings, to deceive with ever elaborate plans — and to rob at their leisure.

This was the early life of Bern Farstrider. He had been that young man, now fallen in with a motley band of brigands. It wasn't the life he had expected, but then it had to be an improvement on the logging camp. That's where his father had worked for most of his life, doing the same drudgery day in and day out. The sons were expected to follow in their father's footsteps, but Bern had no intention of wasting his life. His father had once been a hunter and a woodsman living independently in the wilds. He'd turned his back on that when he got married. Such a life was not right for a wife and a newly born son. Bern realised that his father had exchanged a life of freedom for one that was no better than a cage.

When he was of an age, Bern left with no regrets. Life had been hard since. Not the exciting adventure that he had hoped for, but he'd soon found company in these thieves and outlaws who shared his own desire for thrill and escapade. They were a mixed bag, different ages and backgrounds. Whilst their morals may have been lacking, their skills at survival were not. Bern learned much about tracking and hunting, and living in the wilds. He even discovered he had a good eye with the bow and was soon putting his comrades to shame with his ability to land a shot with ease.

Bern had no desire to change. He lived only for the moment and the next cup of ale. Life was simple and he liked it that way, an outlaw living like a king, and all on his terms. Then everything changed. Their next mark was another noble family with a hunting lodge on the banks of Lake Sorrow. It was late fall and winter's chill already in the air. There would be no one at the lodge save for a caretaker — probably a huntsman who would look after the holding while the nobles were away. Bern and his band had watched the lodge for a couple of days. They'd seen no one enter or leave. It would be unusual for the place to not have at least one guard; else it would fall prey to goblins or other opportunists. Just like them.

There was no need for tricks this time. Bern kicked in the door, an arrow nocked to his bow. The place had definitely been ransacked. Broken chairs and a shattered table, a cupboard dragged on its side, doors open. Clothes and other belongings strewn across the floor. There was blood. A lot of blood. And a knife. Swiftly, Bern and his men checked the other rooms. A similar story. It looked like a tornado had whipped through the place on a rampage of destruction. Bern was the first to spot the claw marks in the wall and across several of the splintered pieces of furniture. The place stank of wolf. One of the windows was broken, its shutters ripped away. They set about filling their bags with whatever few valuables were left unbroken. It was a poor haul but that was just the way it went sometimes.

That could have been the end of it, but then Bern heard the sobbing. It was coming from somewhere nearby, one of the walls perhaps. He tapped the panels, wondering if there was some hidden switch. Then his eyes drifted to the ceiling and the trapdoor above. Dragging over a piece of furniture, he climbed up and pushed on the trapdoor. It opened into a loft area. The ladder had been pulled up for safety. Huddled in the dusty shadows was a young girl, no older than six summers. She was gripping her knees to her chest, frightened and scared. Bern helped her down and tried to question her about her family. The girl was clearly numb with shock. When she saw the blood – she burst into tears, throwing her arms around Bern and clinging to him fearfully. He led her awkwardly from the cabin. The others had little compassion for this newfound burden. She was clearly not welcome.

'Take her to a town and leave her,' said one.

'She will be trouble,' said another. 'People are gonna ask questions.'

Bern grudgingly agreed.

He pulled the girl onto his back and then headed eastwards to the town of Wrenhall. He was intending to do exactly what he had been told, drop her off at a church or some other place of charity, and wash his hands of her. Afterall, she was not his responsibility. However, over the course of the journey, the girl started to open up about what had happened – or at least, what she thought had happened. Bern started to put the pieces together.

Her father had been the caretaker of the lodge. He'd been bitten by a wolf. But no ordinary wolf. He'd used some herbs that should have cleaned the wound and staved off any lycanthropy, but it wasn't enough. When he felt the change, he had to act quickly. He put his daughter in the safest place he could. What happened next, the girl did not know, but Bern was able to guess. The man probably tried to take his own life with the knife, no doubt in fear of what he was becoming. He would have been successful too, but the onset of the change transformed him before he bled out. In the end, he probably bolted from the cabin – made it into the forest. Come morning he would have awoken as a man. And by then, his wounds would finally have taken their toll. Bern didn't share these thoughts with the girl. He saw in her eyes that she knew. Papa was not coming back.

The journey was several days. Bern started to get to know Lizzy and he enjoyed sharing his stories around the campfire – and she was an attentive listener with an inquisitive mind. Bern started to warm to his new companion. By the time they reached Wrenhall, he couldn't leave her – they had formed a bond and his instinct was to father her, to teach her how to survive in this cruel and savage world. And that is what he did. He never returned to his companions. Instead, he built a home – of sorts – within the tangled canopy of the Whisperwood. He taught Lizzy how to hunt and fish, and to shoot with a bow. He'd carve toys and other ornaments to sell at the local market – to make a few coins for luxuries, some candied sweets that Lizzy loved. This was their life. And Bern had the pleasure of watching his adopted daughter blossom into womanhood, now a hardened hunter in her own right and fully capable of handling herself.

Bern had dreaded the moment when they would part ways, but he knew it was coming. He could tell that this life was shackling her, just as his father's had with him. Better that he accept the pain of that loss than make her resent him. One day, they went hunting together – deep into the forest. Bern wanted to test her, check that she was ready to go it alone. The woods were always dangerous. There were many beasts and monsters that could ambush the unwary, not to mention the strange spirits that stalked the shadows, and gave the forest its name. Perhaps it was foolish to trek into the heart of the wood, but even Lizzy seemed compelled that day to push herself to the limits. They scrambled and climbed over tangled roots and through gnarly thickets, warily avoiding goblins and spider dens. What they did find, they could never have been prepared for. They heard it long before they stumbled into its path, drawn by the sound of battle and what sounded like buzzing saws and clanking metal.

The beast was fashioned from iron. A hulking monstrosity that stalked forward on squat legs, shattering logs and roots as it stomped through the undergrowth. The towering body sprouted an array of arms, each one offering a frightening collection of barbed saws and spinning blades. The beast cut a swathe through the ancient forest, leaving a trail of destruction in its wake. Bern would have fled back into the trees – but there were figures struggling to end the golem's advance. Women clad in green-leaved cloth, their skin hued with the colours of the forest. They were firing arrows at the golem, but the shafts were splintering against its iron hide. Bern had heard of the dryads but had never seen one in all his many years. Now, there were seven – darting around the rampaging monster, dodging its blades and saws, and trying to penetrate its armour. They were fighting a losing battle.

Bern drew his bow and started to pepper the thing with arrows, looking for a chink that might expose some critical spot. He had no such luck, but his quick draw and relentless assault drew the monster's attention, and gave the dryads some small respite. It was Lizzy who saved the day. She had clambered up into the canopy and waited for the beast to get close. Then, with a spirited leap, she sprang onto its shoulders. Bern could immediately see her intent. The golem's head was the weakest point. Lizzy balanced on the rocking monstrosity, her blade slamming into the glass-dome that served as a head. It cracked and then shattered, releasing a burst of magical energy. Something flooded out, an elemental of storm and lightning. Lizzy was knocked off, falling into the undergrowth. The beast had stopped its advance, metal arms and legs frozen lifeless. But there was now a raging elemental on the loose. Thankfully, the magics of the dryads quickly brought it down. Bern rushed to Lizzy's side. She was in great pain and he suspected that bones had been broken in her fall. The dryads were melting back into the forest, but one chose to come to their aid. She used some healing tonics on the girl, giving her the strength to stand, although barely. The dryad nodded to Bern and together they supported the girl as they led her to the secluded dryad grove.

At the grove, Bern was to witness his first elder tree – a vast towering structure of leaves and boughs, shining with a majestic brilliance. Lizzy was given further healing for her wounds and a bed of leaves to rest on. It would take her several weeks before she could move without discomfort. Bern spent this time learning some of the dryads' ways, such as the vital bond that they shared with the elder tree. This ancient guardian was coming increasingly under threat. The golem had not been the first – there had been many other vile experiments unleashed on the forest. Their source was a tower to the south, where they believed an archmage was conducting his studies. If he was ever able to create an army of these beasts, then the forest would be levelled in a matter of days.

Bern joined the dryads and together they defeated the archmage and his experiments. They also uncovered the truth behind these monstrosities. The mage had been developing these golems by trapping elementals into bodies of metal. According to his journal notes, he had not been successful in controlling the golems, hence their wild and erratic behaviour. There were clearly other mages mentioned in the notes, who were working on similar projects and sharing their findings – all funded by a mining magnate known as Baron Fromark. The dryads could not leave their grove for long, such was their covenant with the elder tree. Bern agreed to track down these other mages and end their infernal projects. This he did, but without Lizzy's aid, as she had already chosen to take of the sap – and join the dryads in the protection of their grove.

Bern travelled Valeron and, true to his word, he ended the plot to create a metal army of golems that Fromark had hoped would expand his fortunes. During Bern's travels, he met with many dryad groves. His dedication to their cause won him their loyalty and respect. Although he had no intention of taking the sap and losing his beloved freedom, Bern was gifted many powers by the various dryad queens – and was given a rare magical bow, known as the Hornet, fashioned from the wood of an elder tree. In return for these gifts, Bern became a ranger for the dryads, performing missions and errands to help protect the wild places of Valeron.

With the release of the demon known as Jormungdar, the north of Valeron was devastated by seismic upheaval. The Heartlands of Valeron bore the worst of it as a vast fissure ripped across the length of the land, tearing open a vast wound. Many towns and villages were swallowed up into that dark pit, while others were brought to the point of ruin by the many quakes and tremors. Worse was to come, as goblins and other creatures spilled out of the underworld, pillaging and looting – and hampering efforts to rebuild after the catastrophe. There has been little aid from the capital and many people are struggling in the region. Thankfully, there has been talk of a hero who is now offering hope. They call him 'the green hood'.

Bern has been helping many of the smaller villages and hamlets to get back on their feet by fighting off marauding bands of goblins and giving them reprieve. He has taught locals – most of whom are simple farmers – how to use bow, sword and spear to defend themselves. Many settlements have been completely devastated and hundreds homeless. Some have joined Bern, those who have given up trying to recapture their former life, to forge a new one in defiance of the odds. Bern has trained them in the ways of the wild, to track beasts and to hunt. Like his old band that he once ran with in his misspent youth, Bern has now gained a ragtag army of outlaws, who are fast becoming the talk of Valeron as they help this devastated region to recover from its woes.

Betsy Blue – the Queen of the Tides

The moon's brilliance sparkled atop the waves, turning the ocean into a vastness of splintered light. Where the waters rushed ashore, they smacked against the sides of the ships, moored in a forest of many sails. Beyond them, a ramshackle smudge of buildings, clinging to many elevations and fighting for space against a jungle of tree and vine. Here, the moonlight finally conceded to the gaudy blaze of lanterns arrayed across the length and breadth of Clearwater Cay. A small pinprick of humanity, set against the immeasurable void of the Terral Jungle.

At the town's highest point, the tavern known as *The Smiling Skull*, shone the brightest – its string of lanterns picking out the enormous jawbone of a carnosaur, hung over double doors. They opened briefly, spilling raucous laughter and the play of a fiddle out onto the street, along with a drunk who was fumbling with his breeches – then a moment later, relieving himself with a heavy, grunting sigh. Inside the building, a bustling taproom filled to capacity, doing good business as always. Sailors and travellers, and a few locals – a ragtag assembly of patrons from all corners of Dormus.

Davy Jones had command of the top table, spinning another yarn to his attentive listeners, and basking in the glory of his latest endeavour. His crewmates could happily attest to the luck and fine captaincy of Davy the Feared, no greater or more ruthless a sea pirate. A lost treasure was now theirs, and to prove it their gold was rapidly turning from coin to ale as the night wore on. Davy finished his amusing anecdote to rowdy approval, then slouched back in his chair. He called over to the bar for another round. This was a night of celebration. Like the one before and the ones that would come after. This was the pirate's life and no one was going to stop him enjoying it.

The room was hot and stuffy, and full of the stench of unwashed bodies. Mistress Mel stood behind the bar, a former pirate herself. She wore a quizzical frown as she listened to some drunk regale her with his life story. She topped up his glass for the tenth time that night and forced a smile, while gesturing to her barmaid to serve Davy's table. If one was attentive, they'd have suddenly noticed Mel's smile slip, her body stiffening. The drunk continued his rambling, but her gaze had shifted to the doors.

Soon, the others would feel it too. Even those so drunk they could barely stand or remember their name. A cold. A chill, dank cold. Like the depths of the darkest ocean. It washed across the taproom, drowning out the laughter and the music, as if somehow its very presence warranted a respectful silence. A crackle of rime crept across the front doors of the tavern. The fiddle screeched its last note. The last conversation fell to an uncomfortable murmur, a whisper then an expectant quiet. Mel was the only one whose smile had returned. She knew this guest, all too well.

The doors were flung open with a crack of force that almost blew them from their rusted hinges. Standing there was a figure, a pirate to be sure by the tricorn hat and high-collared coat. Mist dripped from her, like the long dark tendrils of hair framing a coal-black face. She stepped into the taproom, walking with a dancer's grace. Where her boots fell, dank water pooled – the creaking of leather punctuated with the rattle of finger bones hanging about her neck. Someone said her name. The noise like a thunder in that deathly silence. The woman gave no response, simply continued her advance, parting a path as those in her way jostled to stay a good distance. Her attention had not drifted for a

second. Those pale eyes, blazing bright as the moon outside, were fixed on one man. He was shifting nervously, his hand inching to the flintlock on the table, then thinking better of it.

She spoke his name. Another thunder in the silence. That was the cue for someone to bolt for the doors. It started a stampede, as drunks and former merrymakers decided that taking the night air was preferable to what was to come. Those around Davy's table had the same idea, but they froze as the woman walked closer. Eyes darted between her and the captain, wondering what exactly was protocol – and how far a contract of loyalty actually went.

The woman was Betsy Blue. A feared legend on the high seas. Everyone knew her tale, or at least some version of it, and the reasons she would come calling. Davy Jones was just the latest of an unsuspecting few, who had fallen foul of the curse – had become the captain of her ship, from which she got her name – *The Betsy Blue*. And everyone knew the price to be paid for sailing that vessel. Davy knew that too, so he dared a smile and shrugged his shoulders. His ship was *The Jackdaw*, so what possible reason could Betsy have with him? But that was all part of the curse. The ship was destined to change hands many times, and change its name too. At times, no-one would know the identity of the ship – not helped by those foolish few who would choose to name their own ship *The Betsy Blue* to gain some notoriety and be part of the story. But they would never get the call. Only those who sailed the real pirate ship of this Sargassi princess.

When Davy realised the truth, his shred of confidence paled to terror. Perhaps his strange luck of late had been part of the enchantments woven into the boards of that accursed vessel. Now he had to pay the price and join Betsy's crew aboard her ghost ship, *The Blood Rose*. Davy reached for his flintlock but never got to fire the bullet. Betsy raised her hand, pale fingers gripped around a glowing compass. Its needle swung to the captain as he levelled his weapon. Then he was gasping for air, his body convulsing. The sailors watched in horrid fascination as their captain was lifted into the air, the dreadful sound of bones snapping and popping ringing in the dread silence. Then from his blue lips, a wisp of smoke clouded into the chill air – his soul essence unravelling from his body. It curled around the compass, spiralling like a whirlpool. Then Betsy snapped the compass closed – and with that motion the essence was gone. The broken body of the captain slapped against the floor, contorted in an agonising moment of death. It had all taken a matter of a few heartbeats.

Betsy pocketed the compass, then her white eyes drifted to the sailors. They looked at one another, then dashed for the door – pushing and shoving each other in their haste to escape. With a grim smile, the pirate queen gave a small shrug, then sauntered over to the bar. Mistress Mel met her smile and placed the mug of salted water on the counter.

'Your usual,' grinned the barkeep. 'Capturing souls can be thirsty work, I imagine.'

Betsy's past is shrouded in mystery and the contradictions of a hundred different tales. It is commonly believed that her real name was once Safi Amardi, the youngest daughter of a previous ruler of Sargassi, Queen Manyara Amardi. According to legend, she fell in love with a Venetian pirate captain and they sailed together, pillaging the southern sea lanes. However, their loyalties were tested when the pirate port of Sheril came under attack by Venetia, who was seeking to control the port and the Cerulean Sea.

The current pirate overlord of Sheril feared losing everything in the conflict. She entrusted Safi and her crew with her gold and her prized belongings, asking that they be taken to a place of safety in case the port fell and was plundered. Safi intended to be true to her word – but her Venetian lover had other ideas. His loyalty was still to his homeland and his trust had been bought, as well as that of most of the crew. They mutinied and in the ensuing fight, Betsy was stabbed and pushed overboard.

The ship, known as *The Betsy Blue*, sailed onwards to Cretaria, where the treasures are still rumoured to be buried to this day. Safi was assumed dead, but – as the story goes – each member of that crew got a visit by a stranger in the garb of a pirate. Their bodies would always be found the next day, lifeless but without a mark or wound, save broken bones as if crushed by enormous pressure. They died one by one, until there was only the captain left – the Venetian pirate who had betrayed his lover. He suffered the same fate. And that doomed crew are now said to serve Safi in death – aboard her ghost ship that travels the dark tides between worlds. What her end goal or purpose is, no one truly knows, but all fear any connection with her ship. For anyone who steps aboard that cursed vessel risks becoming the latest addition to her phantom crew of damned souls.

Conall Bloodmoon – the Crow King

At first it had been a thick fog. Now it was smoke, black and choking – billowing from the burning tents. It obscured the battle, which may have been for the best. It hid some of the horror, but Conall could still hear the screaming. The clash of steel and crackling magic. Somewhere, a woman weeping. He was only seven years old, although he may have passed for older. They said his father was a half giant and he had the same blood in his veins. He was strong and the axe he held was well worn with practice. But this was his first battle and he was paralysed by fear, eyes flitting from one shadow to the next, bodies hurrying through the smoke. It had all been so fast. One moment, eating around the fire as the sun cast the last of its dappled light. Then they had come charging into the clearing. Soldiers in glinting plate and rattling mail. The Wiccan had not stood a chance.

From out of the smoke, some creature strode towards him, a giant of a man – if indeed it was a man. His whole body was aglow, shining brighter than the sun. And his eyes. Conall always remembered those eyes. Not human at all. Piercing orbs of brilliance, shining from behind cloth wraps. He would later learn that this abomination was a paladin. Conall was trembling, unable to move as the giant swung back his mighty warhammer. But the blow never landed. Conall felt the air shifting, suddenly alive with the zip of arrows. Maybe half a dozen pierced that glowing flesh, knocking the paladin back. But somehow, the mighty warrior remained standing, taking wounds that should have killed any mortal. More arrows streaked through the smoke. Then Conall felt the arms settle around him. He looked down. Not arms. They were roots, gnarly and rough. Before he could fight his way free or even register what was happening, the roots yanked him backwards – into the refuge of the forest. Then he remembered no more of that day.

Conall had been rescued by the dryads of the forest. Sadly, their intervention had come too late. There were no other survivors, at least none that Conall knew of. He was the last of the Greenwald clan. The dryads offered what comfort they could, but there was none that could fill the empty void of loss. Conall didn't cry. That was not the Wiccan way. Instead, he felt numb. As if his mind was unable to comprehend the true horror of that day. Later, a man was led to the grove. The chieftain of the Hannon clan. With him was his young daughter, Damaris, probably a summer older than Conall. The chieftain's name was Ladan Bloodmoon and he was well respected amongst the Wiccan. He took Conall as an adopted son and made him a member of the tribe.

Conall grew up to become a great warrior, strong and fearless. With six half-brothers, he was never short of sparring partners or competition. At first, they treated him sourly, calling him a Greenwald runt and giving him more than a few beatings. It was Damaris who told him to stand up for himself. The past didn't matter, Conall was a Hannon now and he needed to act that way and prove himself. With his half-giant blood granting him strength that few others could aspire to, it wasn't long before he was giving back in kind, and his half-brothers were soon forced to accept him as an equal.

Pushed further westwards, the Wiccan found themselves fighting for territory against goblin warbands and ogre marauders. Conall proved himself in battle time after time, winning the respect of the clan and the adoration of Damaris, who had watched him blossom into a mighty champion. They spent many hours together, exploring the woodlands, sharing stories and making up songs of when they would be heroes – and their adventures would be sung around every campfire. On one such journey into the woods, their fates were to be forever changed.

Conall was in his late twenties now and an imposing figure, nearly seven foot in height. Damaris was teasing him as his head knocked into yet another branch, his arms forever swatting at the low-hanging foliage. As they were laughing together, they stumbled into a glade that they did not seem to recognise. Ruins were scattered amongst pools of wildflower, the old stonework cracked and covered in ivy. The place felt ancient and also powerful. Damaris could sense it, as she had already become practised in the druidic arts. This was a crossing point, where leylines met and created ripples of energy. Excited by their find, they explored the ruins. That is where they found the lich. Some ancient being of unfathomable power, hunched on a throne that was half in ruin. Conall raised his axe to strike, but the frail creature only laughed at his show of bravado – a crackling hiss, like splintering ice.

The lich offered them both a wish that it promised to grant. But there would be a cost. A payment. He asked Conall first. The mighty giant searched his heart then gave his answer boldly and without fear. 'To be chieftain.' The lich gave a rictus grin and nodded. Then, the dark hollows of its eyes shifted to Damaris. 'To have power,' she replied. The lich nodded. This time, there was a crack of magic, then a shadowy creature swept forth with grasping claws. After a fierce battle, Conall and Damaris defeated their adversary. As its essence dissipated, Damaris saw the kha lying against the stonework. A throbbing heart of energy, that would give her the dark powers of the creature they had vanquished. Damaris hungrily took the heart. When they looked back at the throne, the lich was gone.

They never found those ruins again, no matter how hard they looked. When Conall returned to the camp, there was weeping and shock. Then he saw the corpses, laid out in a line. The chieftain and his six sons. All dead, looking frozen as if drowned in some ice lake or caught in a blizzard. There were accusations of witchcraft and a curse that had befallen the tribe – all because of Damaris and Conall. But he knew that this was his gift from the lich and he would take it. Any dissenter was quickly silenced, either by fists or axe. No one could match Conall in strength or in arms – and his claim, as an adopted son of the former chieftain, meant his right to lead was sound. Conall became the chieftain of the Hannon clan, with Damaris as his close advisor.

Together they made the clan strong, but life was only getting harder for the Wiccan. Constant battles with goblins and soldiers had forced them into the mountains, where they now took refuge in caves and tunnels, planning their next move. That is when the mercenaries came. They were representing a mining company, that now apparently had a claim on the caves and the surrounding mountains. The Wiccan were asked to leave peacefully. Conall refused to give up their land. In the ensuing fight, he was shot in the chest with a flintlock. The blast silenced the battlefield.

Seeing their leader downed, the Hannon surrendered, outnumbered and outmatched by the magic and firearms of their oppressors. They fled south into the prairies, realising that they no longer had the strength or the numbers to fight back. Conall was dying. No healing tonics would bring him back to consciousness or knit the blackened wound. The shot

had missed his heart, but it was clearly working infection through his body. Unable to help him, Damaris took Conall to the dryads. She left him there in the grove, doubtful even their magics could save him. With a heavy heart, she went south to rejoin her people. They would need to choose a new chieftain and she wanted to be there to give her counsel.

Seven months passed and life only got harder. The prairies were an unforgiving landscape, where little could grow in the stubborn dry earth. Many of the fruits and berries were poisonous, and the wildlife well adapted to defending itself from hunters. A new chieftain had been elected, but Damaris feared he was weak and indecisive. They had lost many to disease, starvation or the dangers of their new land – the future looked bleak for the Hannon.

As Damaris prayed to her old gods, those of the forests and the land and the skies, she sighted the crow perched atop the parched bones that marked the skeleton of some unfortunate beast. The crow watched her, head tilting from side to side. Damaris sensed something. She got to her feet and squinted towards the dusty horizon, where a figure was approaching. As he got closer, her heart skipped a beat – was this some cruel trick of the light, a mirage cast by the unrelenting sun? It was Conall – striding resolutely through the dust, a crow perched atop each shoulder. Strapped across his back was a mighty war axe, sparkling with druidic energies.

Conall had seemingly returned from the grave.

He spoke little of his time with the dryads, but it transpired that – in a last effort to save his life – the dryads had given him some of the sap of the elder tree. This would normally bind a soul to the grove and leave them forever changed. Conall had certainly changed. He had been granted powers beyond that which was mortal. But somehow, he had managed to break the covenant – the enchantment that would keep the tree's servants bound to the proximity of the grove. Perhaps it was his giant blood or just Wiccan stubbornness.

He returned as chieftain. On witnessing the desperate circumstances of his tribe, he vowed to lead them north again. Damaris saw his strength and admired his ability to lead. She suggested they unite all the Wiccan – form one army, united in purpose, then take back what was rightfully theirs. And so, they went north and the plan was started. First, they won back their caverns from the mining corporation, then cleared the surrounding regions of trolls and ogres. Conall's victories drew the attention of the other Wiccan clans, who eventually pledged their allegiance to follow the Hannon.

Despite all of his achievements, Conall became sullen and brooding – often shifting into bouts of melancholy or tempestuous rage. He had taken many wives, as was his right as chieftain, but none had given him a child. He started to wonder if this was his price – the one he had promised to pay for the lich's gift. To die childless, without an heir. And to die having achieved no lasting legacy.

The inquisition had become aware of the threat that Conall posed to the region. They sent their best warriors to capture Conall and bring him to Durnhollow for questioning. Through force of arms and divine magic, they were able to achieve their goal. However, Damaris and the Wiccan had other ideas – and were able to assault the mountain citadel and free Conall. They then set about their bloody revenge, sacking the town of Carvel and taking it as their own.

Damaris was content that they had achieved what they set out to do. Conall was calling himself the Crow King and the town was his to do as he pleased. And yet, he was not sated. He sat his throne with a contemptuous air. The sacking of Carvel had done nothing to satisfy his craving for power. His relationship with Damaris became increasingly strained, until he finally had her taken to the dungeons and chained.

Conall's story may well have ended there, but destiny was not finished with him yet. One day, a stranger came into his hall – a hulking man, almost as tall and broad as Conall himself. When this strange figure removed their hood, Conall saw that it was not a man at all, but an archdemon. It purported to be a prophet and told Conall what the weave of destiny had in store. His words would carry great import. Conall was destined to win the throne of Valeron and through his victory he would gain what he had always craved – a son.

The demon's words gave Conall all the impetus he needed. Now with a Wiccan army under his command, he ranges eastwards towards the capital. Stubborn and dogmatic, he refuses the guidance of Damaris, even though he reluctantly agreed to free her on the archdemon's wishes. Damaris fears that Conall's dogmatic nature will lead the Wiccan to ruin – that somehow, the sap of the elder tree is steadily corrupting him. But his people see only a valiant and storied king, a legendary hero who has sworn to carve out a better future – one that has already begun. Conall will not rest until he has won the throne of Valeron and his murder of crows are screeching his name across Valeron skies.

Eldias Falks – the King's Hound

Considered one of most renowned witchfinders in all of Valeron, this deadly assassin wasn't always destined for such an accomplished career. He grew up on the streets of Assay, just one of many street urchins, abandoned and left to fend for themselves. Life was hard and cruel. By the age of eleven, the boy – then known only by his nickname, Fader, for his ability to give the City Watch the slip – had already taken many lives, some that deserved it and some that probably didn't. He wasn't too bothered about morals. There was no room for regrets on the street. It was survival of the fittest and he wasn't going to lose, even with the cards he had been dealt.

By luck rather than design, he found himself recruited into a gang known as the Crows. They had a bad reputation, even amongst the criminal underworld. Fader didn't care much. Sometimes, you needed to pick a side and having the Crows at your back could never be a bad thing. The jobs were as expected. Extortion, robbery and a lot of killing. It was dirty work but Fader had a real good taste for it and the gang boss appreciated his skills. So much so, that he agreed to take on Fader as his own apprentice and teach him all he knew of the thieving arts. Fader was thirsty for knowledge and soon formed a close bond with his teacher – a father figure he had never had before.

Together, they were soon taking on bigger jobs, pushing the limits of their skills. It almost became an addiction. Soon, the Thieves' Guild took notice and reached out to give them an assignment – a test of sorts, to see if they were worthy of their reputations. The task sounded deceptively easy. Steal a painting. A forgery of little worth, but within the lining of the canvas were smuggled documents. The painting had fallen into the wrong hands at an auction – going to a noble with more money than sense. So, the job was to get in and out, with a minimum of fuss. It looked like an easy win.

When it comes to the Guild, things are never quite what they seem. That fateful evening, things were to take an unexpected turn. Avoiding the patrolling guards was easy, as was gaining access to the interior of the manor. What the thieves hadn't taken into account were the rats that had already sighted them and alerted their master. Fader had no experience of the arcane and was not prepared for what he witnessed that night.

The beast came at them from seemingly nowhere, flashing teeth and fur. Fader was knocked back, momentarily stunned. When he regained his senses, he witnessed the gory mauling of his partner, ripped apart by sharp claws and fangs. The thing was a man-sized rat. Fader went for his daggers. The creature's head snapped round, blood dripping from its jaws. With a snarl, it prepared to pounce. But then a woman's voice halted it. She stepped from the shadows. An elderly woman, grey hair pinned back from an ashen face. Fader went to run, but something held him in place. To his horror, he realised the woman had cast some enchantment on him. He could not move a muscle. He gazed at the rat-thing, fearing he would suffer the same end as his dear companion. It turned out that this matriarch had other plans.

Fader became a prisoner to a household of ratlings – men and women that could transform themselves into rats. He was shackled beneath the house, kept alive with tonics whilst his blood was constantly leeched. He never learned why, but suspected it was used in rituals or potions, he didn't much care. He became little more than an emaciated skeleton, kept in cold darkness with only the squeaking of rats for company. Occasionally, he would be taken upstairs, weak and barely able to stand. He would be paraded around at parties, held on a leash by the matriarch who called him affectionately 'my hound'. He witnessed the corruptness of the noble families and the depraved acts that they indulged in for power and pleasure. Months he endured this torture, until he feared that perhaps he had lost his mind – that this was all some fever dream. No one had come looking for him, not the Crows or the Guild. He feared he would die here – a meal for these rat beasts, not that there was much left to feast on.

It was the Church that eventually came to his aid. Inquisitors had uncovered the ratling nest and had brought their vengeance upon the household. Fader only remembered the woman that day, the light she held aloft on the tip of her staff. At first, he was blinded by those warm, comforting rays – then he saw her face, beautiful and serene despite the horrors she must have witnessed, and that of the broken man she now

looked upon. But there was no shock, or pity or disgust in her expression. Only a loving smile as she placed the palm of her hand on his chest and filled him with a radiance that was like a shock rippling through his body. His weakness had gone, the dizziness and hunger and thirst. In its place a feeling of relief and love. Fader wept for the first time in his life and pleaded with the woman to take him with her.

The woman was Charity Naylor, an acolyte of the One God. She took Fader into her own home, nursing him back to health. During those days, she read to him the scriptures. He started to take an interest, but his real interest was in her. Infatuation was blossoming into love. Once his strength had returned, Fader was given a room at a church hostel, where visiting priests would often stay. In return for his board and lodging, he performed tasks for the bishop and other members of the clergy. In the evenings, he continued to study with Charity, craving any moment that he could spend with her. Through patient practice, he learned about the inner kha – the divine light inside each and every life. To his surprise, he was able to feel and tap into this power, summoning it forth as a light that he could use to both heal and harm.

The name Fader was cast away, along with his former life. He chose the name Eldias, in memory of his Crow teacher. Falks came from a gravestone he would often stop at in the church yard. Some soldier or perhaps clergy. It had a good ring to it. And so, Eldias Falks was born – risen from the ashes of a deadbeat life.

Not long after taking on his new persona, he lost Charity. It had been a church mission to root out a demon cult. Charity had gone along to help provide healing if needed. Only one of the original party survived the battle. Apparently, a demonic entity had been involved – summoned from the chaotic Shroud. Eldias was heartbroken, having lost the one real love of his life. From his grief blossomed a steely resolve. After his own tortures and now this, he realised that he had a calling to serve. He shared his desire with the bishop, who told him about the order of witchfinders and their sworn duty to root out evil. Eldias realised this was what he had been born to do – to marry his newfound divine powers with the street skills of the old Fader.

Eldias was accepted by the Acorlidge in Greyspire and proved adept at his studies. On graduation, he apprenticed with a veteran known as Sol Bardo, and for many years they travelled the lands together, hunting out witches and demons, and other dark creatures. Eventually, Eldias was given the title of master and took on several of his own apprentices. Relentless and unyielding, Eldias lived only for his work. Each vampire he reduced to ash, each demon he cast back to that infernal Shroud, he saw her face – her smile that day in the dungeon. Each fiend that he destroyed was an act of love and revenge. As his reputation spread, he started to take on commissions from the king. An honoured role and one that was highly secretive, as many of those he was now hunting were of noble birth with significant connections.

Whilst on a mission in the Heartlands, Eldias was bitten by a vampire. Fearful of becoming one of the undead, he set about trying to find a cure for his malady. His quest brought him to Blight Haven in the Holy Lands, where he had learned of a tonic that would reverse the curse. Luckily, he was able to save himself before succumbing to his blood lust. However, the experience had left him shaken. The ageing veteran was suddenly less sure of his choice of profession. Perhaps, over time his desire for vengeance had finally been sated, only to be replaced by an unsettling and unfamiliar emptiness.

Eldias has now found solace in the cup, drinking to forget – drinking so as not to face his fears. Often, he will be found in the taproom, recounting his past adventures or passing on his advice for those with an interest. Some say, the great Eldias Falks has gone and will never return. However, every night, no matter his state, he polishes his flintlock and sharpens his blade. Deep down, he knows that one day, Eldias Falks will be needed again. And he will answer that call.

Maria Tremalaine – the Maiden of Antioch

The bards still sing of the dreaming spires of Lull, harking back to an ancient time when the land belonged to the Franks. A time when knights, adorned in splendid plate armour, their colourful banners rippling in the wind, would gallop into battle across the vast green plains and forested hills. It was a time of legend, when great kings were blessed by the enchantress of the lake, and their weapons shone with otherworldly might. What once had been a fledgling kingdom had risen up out of the dark ages to become a thriving and cultured civilisation, with its own arts and architecture, language and writing. Its many towns and growing cities dotted the verdant landscape, rich in its abundance of arable land and mountain ores. Franklin was a land of hope and dreams, and its spired capital was the jewel at its heart.

Then came the hordes from the east. The barbaric tide of Mordland, smashing and destroying with unstoppable force. No knight, no blessed king, no fabled enchantress could withstand the brevity of such a tide. Decades of warfare brought the kingdom to its knees – finally ceding itself to neighbouring Valeron in an effort to survive annihilation. The era of legend was over, but the songs of the dreaming spires would doggedly persist – a lasting legacy of a nation once destined for greatness.

Lull stands as a decrepit remnant of that time, the only settlement to have survived the countless centuries of war. Perched on the edge of the scoured wastelands, its spires still stand proud amidst the bleak and melancholy skies – stretching high as if to escape the stink of what lies below in the rat-infested streets. A few noble families steadfastly cling to old traditions and speak of a time when Franklin will rise again. Their delusions keep them comforted in their walled estates, shielded from the stark reality of the city's morbid decay. Maria Tremalaine was born into such a family.

Raised on stories of past glories, Maria and her two brothers had naïve ambitions of becoming knights like those of legend. They would invent their own stories and adventures, using wooden training blades to act out their battles against fearsome monsters. As they grew older, the Tremalaine children would often sneak out of the confines of their estate to view the soldiers pouring into the city. Lull was often used as a base for the Valeron army, who would stay for a few days to resupply before striking out eastward. They called these excursions a crusade. For three imaginative children, the word evoked the grandness of an epic adventure. Wide-eyed with excitement, they would climb up onto the garrison walls, to watch the army march out into the barren wastes beyond – a landscape now blackened and charred by centuries of battle; nothing like the lush green paradise depicted on the ancient tapestries and paintings. The armies came and they went – but few if any would return. Nevertheless, they drew the admiration of the Tremalaine children – especially the crusaders and cavaliers, with their fortress-like armour, sometimes glistening with runework. These were the modern-day knights, carrying on the legacy of the past. But the Frankish nobles didn't see it that way. Those from Valeron were as filthy and ignoble as the rats that infested the streets. The children would be scolded for their spirited admiration of these warriors, but such punishments did not dampen their zeal.

Reality however, would provide harsher discipline. Another terrible plague swept across the city, as it often did in Lull. The eldest Tremalaine boy contracted the disease and did not survive. When looters broke into the estate, Maria's father and remaining brother were killed before they could make it to the protection of the safehouse. When the plague finally abated, Maria found herself a loner, her mother now a recluse who was prone to fits of paranoia and depression. Without her brothers to bolster her lofty dreams, Maria pushed aside her hopes of adventure and became resigned to a forgettable life within a forgettable city.

Maria had no love of art or books, or any of the pastimes that might have helped her carve out some small career, perhaps as an artist or scribe. She did have some skill with a blade, however – more of an unanticipated consequence of her many years sparring with her older brothers. Seeking to escape her mother's constant attempts at marrying her off to one of her many cousins, she decided to join the Torchlight.

Lull had withstood many Mordland attacks throughout the ages. Somehow, it had always weathered each and every barrage, but its scars were visible for all to see. The city's outer walls had long since fallen and so, what had once been its lower district had now become a ruined and inhospitable dereliction, cut off from the rest of Lull by towering garrisoned walls. This district was now known as the Shambles. The only ones mad or desperate enough to eke out an existence in this ravaged place were thieves, goblins and those too poor or hopeless to better their circumstances. The city watch cared nothing for the lives outside of the inner walls. To them, the Shambles was just another casualty of war – a wounded limb excised from the body.

The Torchlight were a hardy group of veterans, some former city watch, others just disillusioned citizens keen to make a difference. Each night, they would patrol the dangerous ruins, looking to drive out goblin warbands and other scavengers from the waste, and provide food and comfort to those in need. It was dangerous work and many were the tales of a Torchlight party disappearing, never to be seen again. Maria had something of a fatalistic attitude – so such dangers only made her

more determined to sign up. For several years, despite her mother's horror, Maria served faithfully in the Torchlight and honed her skills with blade and shield. One of the men serving in her brigade was an ex-cavalier, who had fought in several crusades out in the wastelands. The experience had clearly damaged him, but his martial talents remained finely honed – talents which Maria was keen to make her own.

During those years, she had witnessed death and suffering. Men and women had died in her arms, nothing like the storybooks or her brothers' tales. These were horrible and painful deaths, bloody and terrible, haunting her dreams. There was no glory in battle or death. Maria thought she had hardened herself to such realities, until her mentor fell in battle to a mob of blight trolls. The loss of her closest friend was a huge shock – and one that led Maria to question her life's path once again.

And so, Maria found herself in the church, praying before the cross of Judah. She had never been a particularly religious person, but her time in the Torchlight had brought her into contact with several acolytes who served in the infirmaries, helping to heal the sick and wounded. Sometimes this would involve their magic – what they called the divine light. Maria had witnessed its miraculous power for herself and it had left an undeniable impression on her. Each and every day, she saw men and women fighting for what they thought they believed in – fighting amongst the waste of a ruined city, where there was only blood, plague, and poverty. But perhaps there was something else – something greater than all of this. A reason for living. Maria poured out her heart in prayer, her grief at her many losses mingling with her angered frustration and confused yearnings. Perhaps, some of her childhood naivety still remained – for Maria had been secretly hoping for some holy light to descend upon her or to experience an inexplicable stirring within herself that would provide a calling. Instead, when she finished her prayer, she found herself alone and unchanged, staring up at the cross through tear-filled eyes.

But perhaps the One God had answered her prayer after all. Footsteps echoed within the vaulted chamber. Maria turned and for a moment thought her divine vision had actually arrived. The woman striding confidently down the aisle was aglow in a soft white radiance, like some living embodiment of the fabled enchantress of

Franklin lore. The woman was a holy paladin, her body inscribed in a thousand lines of scripture. A white band was tied across her eyes, the cloth glowing with the same radiance. The woman stopped, then a smile twitched the scars of her face. This was Verisa Beringard, a veteran of many crusades. Her battalion had arrived in Lull that very morning; just a small force of crusaders, soldiers and mercenaries. They had defied orders to remain at Fort Bastian and were striking out east to reclaim the holy city of Antioch. Some might have called it a doomed campaign, for Antioch had long been rumoured to be lost to the creatures of the wastes. A ruin that even Mordland had lost interest in. But the holy city still had meaning to those of the faith – for Judah himself had planted his rod in the earth and summoned forth a citadel of light, claiming it sacred ground for the One God. What had happened to Antioch since had been a blasphemy that the Church had sought to set right, no matter the cost in money or lives.

Maria believed that this was her calling at last. As she looked upon the strength and majesty of this holy paladin, she was moved to further tears – not of sadness but of joy. At finding a symbol that represented all of her dreams and hopes. An embodiment of a truth that she had long been searching for but never found. Maria fell to her knees before the radiant warrior and pledged her sword and service to the One God. Verisa gladly accepted her offer, seeing within this ardent young woman a semblance of herself back when she still considered herself a mere human.

Maria joined Verisa's battalion and, for the first time in her life, she found herself leaving the city of her birth. Her mother was now being cared for by a relative and showed little interest or concern for her daughter's choice. There was nothing left for Maria in Lull – and perhaps she hoped that Antioch would be the true home that she was searching for; a city that truly lived up to its legends.

Once again, Maria would have her hopes dashed, at least at the outset. The land they travelled through was a broken, ravaged wilderness where mutations stalked the dark and wild magics raged in violent storms. A thousand or more years of war and strife had turned Franklin into a nightmarish wasteland. Its once verdant forests and lakes were now corrupted by blight – oozing with a decay that made the pestilences of Lull pale in comparison. On reaching Antioch, Maria witnessed a whole city that was as devastated as the Shambles. There was nothing left to fight over save crumbling walls, headless statues and weed-choked fountains. And yet, at its centre glowed a tower of white radiance, shimmering like sunlight caught on water. In its exquisite perfection, it stood out in stark brilliance from the devastation around it – and by its very presence, conferred some splendour to the ghost city at its feet.

The streets were a constant battleground. Monsters flooded in from the wastelands, perhaps drawn by easy prey or the light that shone like a beacon across the plains. Pilgrims and crusaders fought side by side, leading a constant mobile war against an ever-shifting enemy. Maria discovered that the holy citadel had been sealed for many centuries. No one had entered or left the building. It was rumoured that only a second messiah, perhaps Judah himself reborn from the weave, could break the seal and enter. And on that day, they would take up the divine rod once again and lead the faithful to salvation.

More stories, more legends. For Maria, it was now about survival. She fought alongside her new companions, clearing out districts and hunting down monsters. It was a long and endless grind with few rewards. Once one area was cleared, another would fall back to chaos. Then a Mordland raiding party would arrive and the battles would escalate. Maria witnessed the true power of the divine light as it tore through the ranks of unbelievers – sometimes as a weapon of holy light, other times manifested as smiting bolts of lightning or glowing auras that would protect and heal. Despite all her efforts, Maria could not find the light within herself. Her attempts only led to frustration, which further distanced herself from the calm meditation and prayer needed to nurture such power. Instead, she relied on the steel of her blade to get the work done – resigned to being a soldier rather than a holy hero.

Even the most stalwart can become jaded. When Verisa lost her faith in saving Antioch, many were stumbled by her decision. They had fought for years within the city, living no better than savages, foraging for food and supplies, constantly warring against monstrous entities and corrupted spawns. A few mages had turned their hands to rebuilding some of the districts, using geomancy to meld the earth and stone into new structures – but even these didn't last for long, as if the very city itself was cursed to never be whole again. Verisa left and many left with her. But Maria was one of those who chose to stay. She had no life beyond the walls of this city and each day, when she looked upon that white tower, she saw something inspiring within its dignity and splendour. Something worth fighting for.

Over the years, the holy ones that journeyed to the city and returned to tell the tale, would speak of the maiden of Antioch. A tireless fighter who led a dedicated battalion of hardened veterans, each honed by their tough existence. Any new detachment arriving within the city would often seek out the maiden – for no one knew the city and its adversaries better than her.

Within the city, life and death was always balanced on a knife edge. Maria knew it was only a matter of time. One day, while on a routine patrol of an area considered secure, she was set upon by corrupted beasts. She survived the attack, but sustained a wound to her arm – a bite that quickly festered. The medics could do nothing to cleanse the infection, not even the divine light had any effect. To save her life, the limb would have to be removed. But it was not a decision Maria got to make. She was lost to delirium and fever, so the matter lay with her medics. When she finally recovered, the relief of survival was quickly quashed by the horrible realisation that she had lost her sword arm.

Maria's only purpose had been to fight. Without her blade, she felt as nothing – worthless. Her battalion still respected her knowledge and wisdom, and urged her to remain as their leader, but Maria was unable to recover from the shock of what had happened. Without telling any of her companions, she left the city – wandering out into the chaotic wastes. She had only one desire. To die. With no food, and a weapon she could barely use now, she marched resolutely towards her inevitable fate. The hills and marshes were the stalking grounds of a multitude of beasts. It would not be long before something chose her as its next meal. Perhaps there was one grand battle left in her – but with only one outcome.

It appeared the weave had other plans. A chill fog washed in across the fenlands, obscuring the landscape. Maria found herself trudging blindly through the brackish waters. Tired and without hope, she finally fell to her knees – and for the first time in many months, she prayed. Not for forgiveness or aid, but for a quick death and a release from her despair.

When she opened her eyes, she saw the light approaching, its brilliance parting aside the mist. It was a hooded figure, slender and tall, their robes shimmering with the same radiance that shone at the centre of Antioch. Maria squinted into the light, seeing the sword that rested on the stranger's outstretched palms. She felt no fear, only confusion – and wonderment. When the figure spoke, it was a woman's voice. She implored Maria to take the sword – the blade of kings long past, given back to the waters but now raised up again. Maria put out her one hand, but the stranger drew back, insisting she use her other. Maria could only scowl, thinking it a mockery of her maimed state. But the stranger was insistent, telling her to will her arm to take the sword.

Anger, self-loathing, and the fierce faith that had once driven her, rose to the surface – and with those tumbling emotions, something was drawn out from deep within. It felt like a glow, a warmth she had never felt before. As she strained with her mind, from her shoulder poured a phantom light, shaping itself into an arm and a hand. She could feel it as surely as if it was of flesh and bone – a limb born of the divine light. In awe, she guided her hand to the grip of the blade, fingers closing tightly around it. At that moment, the stranger vanished, the light winking out of existence. But within Maria's grasp was left a very real sword – an ancient blade carved with the names of the Frankish kings. A blade of legend.

'Return to Antioch,' whispered the stranger's voice. 'And break the seal of the citadel. For you have been chosen.'

Saul Ravenwing – the Protector of Valeron

The Ravenwings are a prominent family from Talanost, that can trace their ancestry back to the days of Perova, when the land was ruled by undead. Stories tell how the Ravenwings aided the Valeron conquest of the land, when the Church pushed south to defeat the last vampire lord and torch the cursed city of Perova. Since, then they have always sat prominently in the affairs of Talanost, helping to rebuild the city after the first legion invasion– and defend it from future threats.

Saul Ravenwing was born in 1318 of the Ascendent. His father was serving as the captain of the Talanost militia. It was tradition for the sons and daughters of the Ravenwings to become soldiers or serve in some military capacity for the city. However, Ancelot Ravenwing always wished for a different fate for his youngest son. He saw in him a potential that his other children lacked – a curiosity and worldliness that perhaps would be better served beyond the confines of city walls.

Saul did not have such dreams. He wanted to be like his father and defend his family's homeland.

As soon as he was of age, Saul joined the militia and was content to act as a soldier and watchman for the city. However, several years later, when the city of Merino fell under attack by an army of giants and goblins, he joined a relief force that would attack the monsters from the rear. During that battle, Ravenwing proved his valour many times, finally besting the cloud giant king and routing the goblin horde. It was a bittersweet victory, for his father had been mortally wounded in the battle. As he lay in his son's arms, he implored Saul with his last dying breath that he forget the militia and become a knight and protector of the realm.

Following his father's funeral, Saul had hoped to honour that wish. He asked his family whether they would be willing to sponsor him for the king's academy. His mother refused, thinking it abhorrent that one of their family would turn their back on Talanost – their home – and train to be a Valeron knight. In truth, she feared losing him. Out of all her sons, Saul was most like his father. As for his siblings, they thought him arrogant and foolish, with ideas above his station.

Fate was soon to intervene. Saul had earned the named 'giant slayer' for his role in the Battle of Merino and had become something of a local celebrity. He had been promoted to captain of the Talanost militia, the youngest to ever hold that position at the age of twenty. Word would soon reach the king's ears of this young soldier's achievements. As a war hero himself, Leonidas wanted to meet with the man that could best a cloud giant in combat and win over the hearts of so many.

Leonidas sent a messenger to Talanost, requesting that Saul visit the capital as part of a commendation ceremony in his honour. His mother naturally voiced her dissent, but Saul wanted to go so that he could speak of his father's sacrifice and ask that his father be honoured in his stead. With this, his mother finally gave her blessing. Saul travelled to the capital and was granted audience with the king. On his arrival into Assay, he was surprised to witness the crowds that had gathered in the streets – calling his name and gifting him titles such as 'giant slayer' and 'raven of Valeron'.

At the ceremony, Saul uncomfortably accepted the many plaudits and accolades given to him, but he was only biding his time – waiting for his moment. When it came, the hall fell silent as the young and nervous soldier stood to address those assembled. He spoke from the heart, giving an earnest account of his father's life and how it was Ancelot that had always inspired him. He spoke of their final battle together on the plains outside of Merino – a tale that would go on to be repeated and embellished many times in the taprooms of Valeron. Saul had hoped to shift attention away from himself, but his speech only drew further praise. As well as a hero, he was now seen as the doting and honourable son – the perfect role model. Word quickly spread throughout the city. Saul had inadvertently become a number one celebrity.

If Saul had hoped for a quick return to Talanost, then he was to be disappointed. He was immediately made a captain in the king's army and asked to help lead a campaign into the troll country to end a rising threat. This was to be the first of many assignments. Each one he performed only cemented his reputation for military brilliance and shrewd tactics. There were many more campaigns, each one more dangerous and challenging than the last. Saul always returned victorious, with the minimum of casualties and peace restored. He was not only winning over the general populace, he was also fast-becoming a respected figurehead within the army – admired by knight and soldier alike. Saul cared not for such plaudits. Each assignment he accepted, he hoped would be the last – so that he could finally return home to Talanost.

Leonidas had no intention of letting his famed champion go. By now, his first-born son, Malden, was in his teenage years. The king feared that, without a steady hand to guide him, Malden would fall in with the corrupt nobles of the city, throwing away a promising career in the military for a life of gambling, partying and decadence. He chose Ravenwing to be his son's mentor; to train him and to be the father figure that he needed, just as Ancelot had been to Saul. Leonidas had once been a veteran on the battlefield – a king that liked to lead from the front. But now, in his ageing years, he was frequently sick and often bedridden. He knew he was not the one to instil the right values in his son. Only Ravenwing could do that.

The two were to become inseparable friends. And just as Leonidas had hoped for, Saul became the inspiration that Malden needed to help him stay focused and aspire to greatness. They fought together in many campaigns – and word soon started to spread that Malden was 'the young raven', a hero in the making, who would one day be as great as the valiant Saul Ravenwing.

By now, Saul had been promoted to general – but he had always remained a humble man who shirked attention or honours. He was always focused on the job at hand and anything else was a needless distraction. Malden was of a different mindset. His popularity was making him arrogant. He was drinking more than he should and practising his craft less. Several times, he disobeyed orders on the battlefield, putting his own battalions in danger due to his recklessness. During an ill-fated campaign into the Contested Lands, Malden was severely wounded and, despite the best efforts of the medics and chaplains, he lost his right leg and became a cripple. His military career was over.

Malden blamed Ravenwing for everything, even though it had been Malden's foolhardiness that left him exposed. Nevertheless, Saul took what had happened to heart and wished for time away from the battlefield. Leonidas granted him his wish and allowed Ravenwing to return to Talanost – not only to take on leadership of its militia, but to also act as advisor to the governor who had recently taken on the position. Saul gladly accepted.

That governor was Ellis Harkat, a widowed baroness of Frankish decent. Her appointment to governor had been frowned upon by the Talanost nobility, but she was a fierce and confident woman – and shrewd when it came to playing the political game. She quickly won the heart of Saul, who saw in her something of his own tactical aptitude and fearlessness. Likewise, Ellis had finally met a man who had a good heart as well as a hero's reputation. The two were soon married and had a son, who Saul named after his father, Ancelot. Unlike Saul, the boy had an affinity for magic. Keen that he get the right instruction, Saul called on a contact at the university – a powerful archmage known as Avian Dale. The two had become friends since Saul's return to the city, both having served for their king and country. Avian made the necessary arrangements to have Ancelot accepted by the university so that he could train and master his arcane skills.

Ravenwing would remain in Talanost for most of his advancing years – working to keep its regions safe and patrol the roads south to Merino and Salvation. He may have hoped to grow old gracefully, but that was not to be. With the opening of the Shadow Gate, a demonic legion poured into Talanost. Suddenly, the city needed its hero again – and Ravenwing proved to be up to the task. Together with Avian Dale, he hatched a plan to evacuate the entire city, then placed a magical barrier around it to contain the demons within. His standing army was small and they needed reinforcements. The king's army would take a week or more to arrive. The odds were bleak, but Saul refused to give up hope, even though victory seemed forever out of reach.

Then things got worse. A vile necromancer known as Zul Ator raised an army of undead from the tombs and crypts north of Talanost. He was planning to break through Ravenwing's forces and destroy the mages that were channelling the shield. If he was successful, then the demons would be free to rampage throughout Valeron, spreading destruction and ruin. Thankfully, Ravenwing was made aware of this second threat and was able to head it off and vanquish the necromancer.

During the battle, Saul fought side by side with a Nevarin – one of the shadowborn agents that would ordinarily serve the legion. Except, this one had turned traitor. Many wanted the Nevarin killed, refusing to trust that he was loyal to their cause. But Saul saw a truth in the man's heart and knew he was genuine. In secret, he let the Nevarin enter the city, dropping a section of the shield for only a few moments. His trust proved well placed. The Nevarin was instrumental in closing the Shadow Gate and helping to end the legion's plans. Saul had hoped to sing this hero's praises, as he had once done his father's. But he was never given that chance – the Nevarin was lost during the fighting as his forces sought to secure the last regions from the demon infestation.

Talanost is a city of ruins. The refugees have fled south to Merino, where they have now formed a ragtag camp around the city's walls. The city guard are refusing anyone entry, after looting and other crimes have plagued the city. Despite the battle being won, few of the former Talanost populace are keen to return to the demon-ravaged wreckage. The mages have already started to recover some of the magic items and tomes from the demolished university, but the situation has naturally proven difficult to police. The lure of a recently-sacked city has drawn other more unsavoury types – treasure seekers and thieves, as well as bands of marauding monsters, keen to pillage what they can from the ruins. Adventurers and mercenaries are already flocking to the city to lend their aid to the floundering militia.

With the news of the king's murder, and that of his sons – Ravenwing has returned to the capital. His presence has not been welcomed by Cardinal Rile. Saul never displayed any love for the Church, having found the inquisition a constant thorn in his side during his campaigns. Often these holy warriors would try to undermine his authority or inadvertently spread dissent amongst the ranks of his soldiers. Naturally, he is now suspicious of foul play. Rile remains insistent that Mordland is to blame for the murders. Saul has tried to investigate these claims, but has been thwarted at each and every turn. This has given him further reason to doubt the validity of the tale.

There is believed to be no rightful heir to the throne – at least not one that could be proven legitimate. Ravenwing suspects otherwise. His former friendship with Leonidas had given him access to a lot of private information and gossip. One of these conversations has been gnawing at his mind: a tale of a royal family and their alleged untimely demise. There was a loose end. A life not accounted for. Perhaps this might lead to the rightful heir – someone that the people could unite behind. All he had to do was find her...

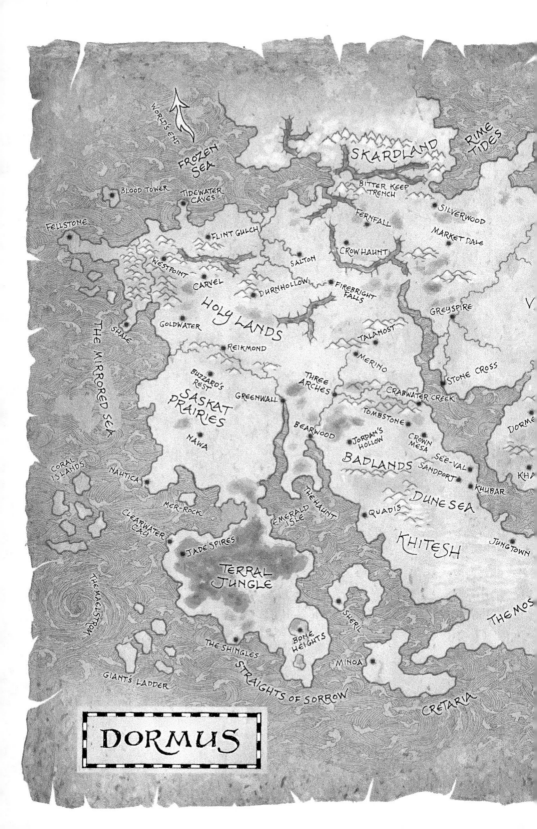

DORMUS

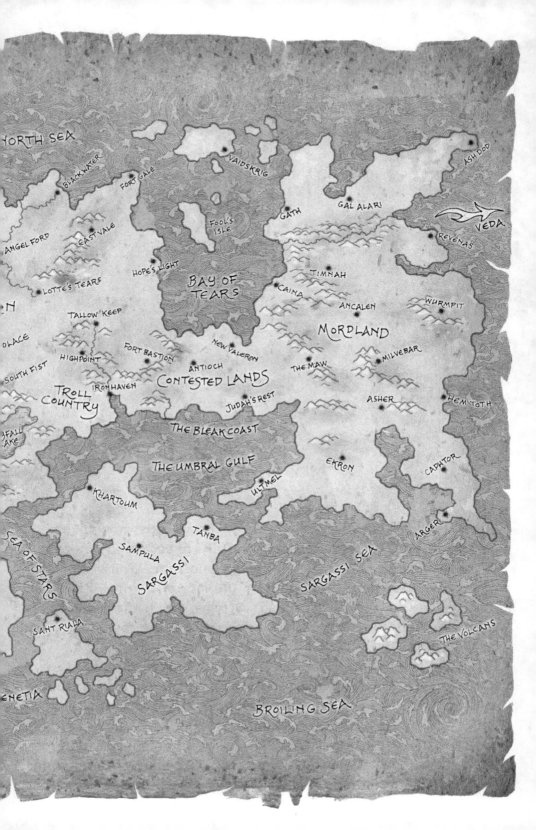

8
Atlas of Valeron

From its origins as a molten fire-world, Dormus has now bloomed and flourished thanks to the elemental gifts of earth and water that Kismet channelled into the once barren landscape. Whilst the elder races have long since vanished from the face of Dormus, its lesser races have thrived and expanded, carrying within themselves the vital seed of destiny that Gabriel gifted them at the cost of his own existence.

As the last surviving world of the three celestial Fates, the lesser races have a key part to play in the destiny of the universe. Judah spoke of a future age of enlightenment, when mankind would put aside their grievances and join together in harmony, to further the plans of the One God rather than their own. Alas, such an optimistic vision has yet to be witnessed. Now more than ever, the nations of Dormus are riven with bitter rivalries and competition – and nowhere is this more evident than in the nations of Valeron and Mordland.

Both these world powers vie for control of land and resources, aware that any small advantage gained by one nation could tip the balance inexorably in their favour. Mordland has been clever in its alliances, absorbing new allies into its realm to serve its devious purposes. In contrast, Valeron has been looking increasingly inwards, trying in vain to regain its strength and identity as a kingdom – as the splintering of its society continues to fracture any shared bond of nationalism.

Nevertheless, Valeron still lays claim to vast swathes of land. Some of these have been won as the result of conquest, others are simply markings on a map with no real physical presence to prove any ownership – only that such regions are less desirable to other nations, who have yet to seek to conquer them.

The following atlas provides details on the major region zones that form the current Kingdom of Valeron, as well as notable places of interest and world lore.

The River Country

Valeron owes much of its success as a kingdom to the challenging landscape of its interior – a land fed by many rivers, which branch and twist into a myriad of channels, creating vast swathes of marshland and bogs. Neither the former kings of Amaral or Franklin could gain any foothold in Valeron, battling against those who had long since adapted to the rain-drenched wetlands. These Valernese tribes could easily lead their foes to ruin, either through the fast-manoeuvring of troops along the river channels or leading their enemies into sludgy mires that could trap and drown whole armies. In later ages, even the might of Mordland fell victim to this wilderness, its fast-moving cavalry encumbered by the swampy grasslands and unable to put up a spirited defence against the hit-and-run tactics of the Valeron army.

Whilst the land has offered up many challenges, the main rivers that cut through the landscape have proven to be its lifeblood, sustaining the development of cities and towns by allowing the swift movement of trade by water as well as by land.

To the east and south, travel becomes more demanding as few of the roads are maintained and most of the navigable routes are little more than muddy tracks and trails. In truth, this has been a calculated policy on behalf of both the king and Church to limit any advance of an encroaching enemy from the east – as Mordland has historically been viewed as Valeron's main rival. However, this may have been a foolish oversight, as a new enemy is ranging in from the west – a Wiccan army that is moving rapidly across the Heartlands with its eyes set on the capital. Such a route is significantly more navigable, although recent seismic upheaval in the west may have ironically played into Valeron's hands by delaying this new threat to the realm.

Assay: At one time the capital of the realm was little more than a fishing port hugging the shadows of a crumbling walled keep, where the first king of Valeron had staked claim over a kingdom. Following tradition, future kings continued to call the town of Cairns their home – and nurtured its gradual expansion into a city as trade and population boomed. However, centuries of war had left the city little more than a squalid has-been, clinging onto a paltry existence at the head of a failing kingdom. Then Judah, the messenger who carried Gabriel's holy light to Valeron, miraculously changed its doomed destiny thanks to a prophetic claim. He revealed to the king that a vast source of wealth lay untapped in the hills outside of the city walls – and true to his word, an abundant source of gold, platinum and silver was discovered. These valuable resources were pivotal in restoring the city to prominence, and earning its new name 'Assay' as a stamp of both its material and divine approval. Today the city is a sprawling metropolis with two faces – that of the wealthy and that of the poor. The old walled city is a haven for the rich

RIVER COUNTRY

and influential, where its streets are regularly policed by the city watch and inquisition, and its privileged nobles enjoy a life of decadence and political manoeuvring. Beyond those walls, where the sprawl spreads like a malaise along the Broadway River, the divide is evident – with cramped streets of tumbledown buildings and refuse choked alleyways. Here, the street gangs and petty crime lords hold sway, black markets sell their illicit wares in river-side warehouses, and reputations are won and lost in the gambling dens and fighting pits.

Solace: Also known as 'The White City' or 'The Pious City', Solace gained its early fame as the site of the White Abbey – a grand and ambitious project that was approved by King Hemides to serve as a symbol of hope following many years of hardship and civil war. This cathedral would become the spiritual home of the appointed heads of the Church, Lord and Lady Justice, and the white abbots who would perform the rites to create anointed paladins and inquisitors. Since those early days, the city has expanded, largely due to the wealthy gentry moving away from the squalor and crime of Valeron's other major cities, such as Blackwater, Greyspire and Kiln, to a better life within a flourishing community of artists, craftsmen, freethinkers and idealists. The walled city functions as a gated community, with curfews and the inquisition maintaining a tight control over who is let in and out of the city. Its avenues are lined with theatres, arenas, jousting fields, opera houses and tea parlours – and high prices ensure that only the rich can enjoy such pleasures – as well as the ostentatious all-night parties that go on behind closed doors once the curfew bells ring. The nearby town of White Flow, which hugs the banks of its namesake river, provides much of the service industry, which travels to and from the city as required.

Kiln: Visitors to Kiln would be greeted with a cityscape of chimneys and factories, spewing their chemical fumes into the sky and shrouding the city within a perpetual smog that rarely parts way for sunlight. Built over a group of underground magma pools, the resulting steam is fed through a myriad of pipes, vents and tunnels, to fuel the enormous machines that work day and night to produce cotton, wool, steel and machinery. The hum and rattle of the vast factories is the heartbeat of the city and its ever-expanding workforce, poorly paid and forced to endure torturous hours of labour, are the lifeblood that keeps the machines running and the profits rolling in for its wealthy overlords. Beyond the city's blackened walls, the land carries the scars of its alchemical crimes, with rivers turned to toxic sludge and the land itself recoiling as its plants and wildlife either perish or become corrupted by its blight.

Highpoint: Situated on the slopes of the Cloudreach Mountains, the town of Highpoint is famous for its griffon trainers who tame these exotic mounts for use within the Church and the Valeron army. The town's 'cloud rangers' are skilled mountaineers, capable of scaling the vast heights to reach the secluded griffon eyries, subduing any territorial males (that are often left to guard the nests while the mother hunts) and procure one or two of the eggs. The remainder are left to hatch in the wild, to ensure a new generation can flourish. These eggs and their hatchlings are highly prized, and occasionally find their way onto the black market, but such instances are rare as the cloud rangers also police the area and serve as guardians for the preservation of the species.

Hope's Light: Once an unremarkable fishing town known as Crowfoot, this backwater settlement had an uncertain future following a period of persistent Vaidskrig raiding. However, its fortunes changed overnight when a mysterious stranger arrived on their shores and began to preach a message about the One God. That stranger was Judah, the messiah who would go on to become a legendary hero and figurehead for a new faith. Following Judah's martyrdom and the later teachings of his apostles, the storied places related to this venerated hero became holy sites – drawing flocks of pilgrims eager to seek out any physical landmark that would give credence to his existence and message. As such, Crowfoot became a thriving hub and was later renamed Hope's Light to reflect its newfound status. Inevitably, the town now has its fair share of charlatans, selling trinkets and souvenirs, and trading stories of those whose ancestors were allegedly there and spoke with Judah when he first made his appearance. Nevertheless, there is still a thriving fishing population within the settlement, who continue to ply their trade around the Bay of Tears, and supply fresh seafood to the many bustling taverns and eateries along the seafront.

The Heartlands

Once the former kingdom of Amaral, the fertile hills and dales of the Heartlands are also known as the 'breadbasket' of Valeron, providing the kingdom with its essential crops and resources. The rich arable land has been a constant boon to farmers, whilst the many verdant forests offer up an abundant supply of lumber and fuel. Much of the landscape is dotted with patchwork farmland and logging camps, whilst sizeable mining ventures tap the rich veins of ore and minerals in the northern mountains. Where the land turns to rolling hills and plains, animal breeders and trainers have set up successful ranches, rearing some of the finest breeds of work horses and war horses outside of the Saskat Prairies.

Recent seismic upheaval has thrown this region into chaos, with a huge rift, known as the Sunblight, ripping a scar across nearly 200 miles of territory. Many villages and hamlets were swallowed up by the enormous crevasse, whilst those that have survived are mostly left in ruin – their efforts to rebuild now hampered by raiding parties of goblins, trolls and other nefarious creatures that have crawled up from the underworld. In the north, several devastating tsunamis have struck the coastal regions, leaving much of the area around the former town of Silverwood a sodden marshland.

The inhabitants of the Heartlands are ignorant of the events that have led to this devastation, but those of a zealous nature have been quick to turn to religion as an explanation for the region's woes – believing that a lack of faith has brought about this divine punishment. Others are convinced these events herald Judah's prophesied 'end days' and fear for the future of the kingdom.

Market Dale: There is a popular saying, 'all roads lead to Market Dale'. Situated close to the border between the Heartlands and the River Country, this thriving city enjoys prominence as a popular gateway between western and eastern Valeron. Farmers and craftsmen from throughout the Heartlands channel their produce through this city, where its many markets and plazas are always abuzz with trade. Many are drawn to its cobbled and crowded streets, including mercenaries and adventurers, who often find work escorting merchant caravans to their destinations. The city's inns and taverns offer a rich source of news and gossip from all corners of the land, while its many festivals, linked to

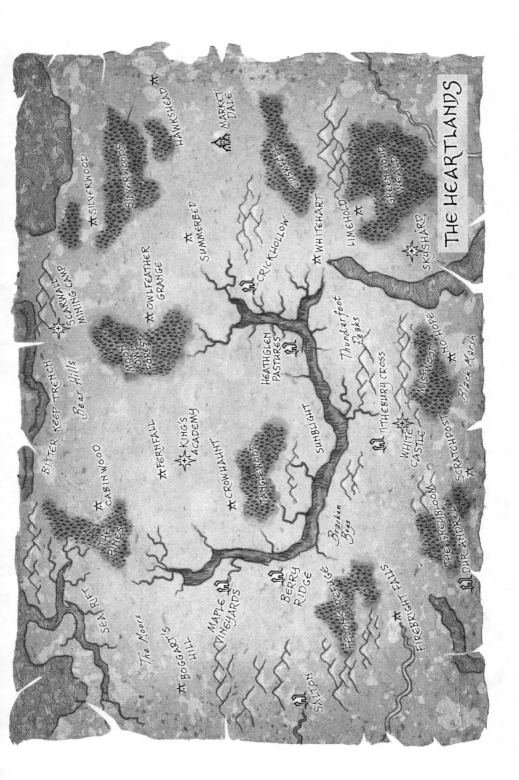

the farming calendar, often draw tourists and pleasure seekers from the outlying cities. Whilst some of its buildings and walls have collapsed as a result of the seismic upheaval, it has fared better than other settlements in the region. However, the city's governor (Duke Peringlad) has so far failed to provide assistance to outlying towns and villages, and instead focused efforts on rebuilding his own city's walls.

Whitehart: Nestled atop the limestone cliffs that overlook the Cerulean Sea, Whitehart is a small fishing town named after the white-tailed deer often sighted in the surrounding hills and woodland. An elaborate lift system provides access to the shale beaches along the coastline, where fishermen and beachcombers have access to an abundant source of seafood, from crabs, winkles and muscles, to the popular silverhead trout. Hunters and explorers often use the town as a base when venturing into the verdant expanse of the Greengold Weald or the tangled depths of Duskfell forest.

No Hope: Where the forested land recedes into the stagnant waters of Black Marsh, the ramshackle town of No Hope clings desperately to a meagre existence. Built on a series of rickety walkways that web across the marsh, this strange haven has always been something of an oddity. Originally founded by a coalition of hunters and alchemists from the Botany Society, the settlement developed from a small camp into a sizeable town as other trades and services settled and thrived, due in part to the rich finds amongst the sunken ruins of the marsh. Over the years, the town has both boomed and waned, based on the fickle fortunes of those who scour the wilds for its treasures. Much of the marsh has now been explored and plundered, meaning the town has largely been left to rot. This has led to the locals renaming the town 'No Hope' in mockery of its original title – New Hope. Nevertheless, there are many who still choose to eke out a living in this remote corner of the kingdom, whilst those looking to lie low and escape unwanted attention find its ramshackle streets a welcome refuge.

King's Academy: Set up by King Remis for the training of elite knights, the academy has garnered a well-earned reputation for producing high calibre graduates. Study involves three years of rigorous training in all aspects of warfare, from weapons and horsemanship, to tactics and military history. Graduates often go on to apprentice with a noble house or notable individual for a further two years of service, before typically accepting a position of standing within the Valeron army. Whilst most of those who attend are from noble stock due to the costs and competition for places, a few commoners with noticeable talent can be granted a scholarship from a special fund set aside by Avian Dale, known as the Grandmaster's Fellowship Fund.

Skyshard: Following a particularly violent storm, a hunting party from Whitehart stumbled on a series of green-veined rocks peppering the hills and valleys of this southern region. Pulsing with strange energies, these rocks defied all explanation and proved unbreakable to pick or axe. The largest of these rocks has been named the 'Skyshard' due to its dagger-like appearance, the jagged length piercing clean through a rocky outcropping. The locals steer clear of the area, aware of the strange mutations and anomalies that are now occurring in the surrounding flora and fauna. Recently, the Botany Society have taken an interest in the rocks, and have requisitioned an abandoned tower in the vicinity to use as a base for their studies.

Perova

From fog-shrouded forests to bleak, windswept moors, the region formerly known as Perova still carries terrible scars from its past. Once ruled over by powerful vampire lords and liches, the haunted ruins and shadowed vales still cry out with the despair of anguished spirits, unable to find rest.

Thanks to a zealous campaign launched by King Bevan in 372 of the Ascendant, Valeron finally defeated the last of Perova's malign rulers, putting its ancient capital to the torch. Freed from its subservience to dark masters, the people could now look forward to a better life under Valeron rulership. New settlers were encouraged to move into the territory, especially those of a religious persuasion, as a means of spreading the word of the One God to Perova's pagan people. Many new settlements were founded, such as Whitechurch and Salvation, whilst the crumbling war-torn cities of Talanost and Merino, were restored to some semblance of their former glory.

Despite the best efforts of its people, the land has always remained a gloomy realm, where travel can be perilous for those who are unprepared. Wolves prowl the forested hills, while witches and warlocks conduct dark rituals in the spirit-cursed ruins; even the swirling fogbanks have been known to take on a sentient malignance, claiming victims who are never seen again.

Perova: The former capital of the ancient kingdom of Perova was put to the torch by the inquisition. All that remains of the city is soot-blackened ruins. Due to the dark and bloodthirsty history of the place, none have sought to rebuild and settle upon such cursed land. The bleak ruins and dark cliffs that overlook the sea are now known as 'The Haunt', and are avoided by all but the foolhardy. According to legend, there is a vast series of catacombs and tunnels beneath the former city. Many ship captains travelling into the Noose, have reported seeing lights within the ruins as well as in the crevasses and caves of the wind-lashed coastline, suggesting that someone or something is still active within the region.

Talanost: The recent invasion by the Legion of Shadow has left the city devastated. An army garrison is now supporting what remains of the city watch, under the leadership of captain Vergus Stoica. Looting is rife amongst the ruins, especially within the previously wealthy districts and the former University of Magic. A magic delegation is now seeking to retrieve as much as they can from the devastation, although their efforts have been hampered by the violent elementals now unleashed from their bonds. Monsters from the surrounding hills have also moved in to pillage and prey upon the beleaguered inhabitants, making efforts to rebuild that much harder. In response, mercenaries and adventurers have been welcomed by the garrison, to help with the reclaiming and renovation of the city.

Merino: When Talanost fell to the Legion of Shadow, those that managed to escape the ensuing carnage fled south to the city of Merino. Arriving in their many hundreds, the governor of the city closed his gates to the refugees, refusing them entry to the city. In response, the refugees have been forced to build their own ramshackle camp outside of the city walls. Despite some aid being provided from

THE GREY MARSH

THIMBLE HILL

DOUR GAUN

DOUR PEAKS

SEEKER'S HOLLOW

DRAGON ROOST

TOLDARK KEEP

COAL MOUNTAINS

Bone Fields

BARLAD

MERINO

TALANOST

Blighted Lands

WEBWOOD

Hungry Hills

SALVATION

WITCH'S DELL

BLACK STINE

Merino River

GREENWALL

TORVIL MINING CAMP

THREE ARCHES

PEROVA MOUNTAINS

The Wall

WHITECHURCH

RUSHWATER

NAILING WOOD

Gallow Hills

BEARWOOD

LAKE SORROW

WRENHALL

The Noose

Bad Lands

WHISPERWOOD

PAROVA CRYPTS

The Haunt

PAROVA

PEROVA

the inhabitants of Merino, the Talanost people are suffering from malnutrition and disease. There has been fighting and rioting, and the city watch has been forced to take on mercenary companies to help them man the walls and prevent breaches into the city. The governor has been pressing Valeron's new regent for aid with the situation, but no help has been forthcoming. Some of the refugees have chosen to return to Talanost, seeking to reclaim their former lives, however they face even greater challenges within the ruins of that fallen city. Stories of such trials have only served to deter those who are still encamped at Merino, now desperate for some relief from their suffering.

Whitechurch: The buildings in Perova are typically fashioned from the black stone and slate that is common to the region. This can bestow a dour and brooding look to its villages, towns and cities. When Valeron started to settle in the newly-conquered lands, the pious people who founded this settlement desired to build their church from granite, believing that the black Perova stone would be an affront to their deity. The granite was transported from the eastern mountains – and the ensuing structure served to give the settlement its namesake.

Bearwood: This once unassuming settlement began as little more than a logging camp. However, the ample resources within the region, from its lumber to the furs and pelts of its abundant wildlife, has allowed the settlement to expand into a thriving port, and one of the largest on the South Sea. Goods coming into Bearwood are less regulated than those at Stone Cross and Greenwall, meaning that it has garnered popularity with smugglers and black-market traders, looking to move illicit goods, from spices and exotic animals, to demon khas and even slaves, into the interior, via the Blackmoor River.

Greenwall: Sometimes known as 'The Hanging Gardens', the city of Greenwall is believed to have been built on a powerful crossing of leylines. Legend has it that its founder was a druid, who built a settlement to honour the fallen guardian of the grove, an elder tree that was put to flame by a dark sorcerer. Whether there is any truth in such claims is not known, but what is plain to the eye is the workings of druidic magic in the city's earth and stone, as if some powerful natural enchantment is still exercising its will. Many of the city's buildings are covered in natural foliage, making the city appear almost as one with its surroundings. The inhabitants have learned not to fight against such magic but to nurture it – and now its many streets and gardens are ablaze with colour as a result of the many trees and flowers that feed off the natural vibrancy of the land. Greenwall's location has allowed it to thrive as a seaport, although Bearwood has started to steal much of its trade and standing in recent years. Nevertheless, there is no shortage of travellers who flock to the city to witness its floral beauty – and perhaps catch a glimpse of its legendary guardian known as 'The Green Man', a powerful wood elemental, who is occasionally sighted on the rugged hills between the city and the Webwood.

The Holy Lands

At one time, the western reaches held little interest for the kings of Valeron. It was seen as a heathen land, where only brigands and savages could eke out a meagre existence amidst its brackish fenlands and bleak moors. For the Wiccan people, this was their home – known from ancient times as Gilglaiden. Its harsh and unyielding terrain was seen as a boon to a people who wished to deter outsiders, and be left untouched from the warring factions and politics of the world at large.

Sadly, that all changed when the prophet Allam Medes, the youngest son of King Gerard, started to have visions of a light in the west. Convinced that it was a sign from his god, and with the fervent backing of the Church, Allam was positioned at the head of a holy crusade, to claim the lands for the crown.

The Wiccan fought fiercely for their lands, with many tribes refusing to bend the knee to a king they did not recognise or a god they did not believe in. Unable to stand up to the might of the Valeron army, dozens of clans were wiped out or forced to surrender. Others were expelled from their lands, the barrows of their ancient heroes and chieftains left undefended as they sought desperate solace in the deep woods or the mountain caves.

Since the conquest, Valeron has claimed Gilglaiden as its own and renamed the region 'the Holy Lands' in remembrance of Saint Allam. But the bitter wrongs that have been wrought on the Wiccan people run deep – and now a spirited rebellion has been kindled, under the leadership of Conall the Crow King. Many tribes now flock to his banner, seeking revenge for the atrocities that they have endured.

Carvel: The town of Carvel was once a popular destination for pilgrims, seeking to pay their respects to Saint Allam and his sainted knights, whose bodies are interred beneath its church. However, the town was the first to be sacked by Conall and his Wiccan army when they went on the rampage. Only a lucky few were able to escape the slaughter. Hundreds were put to the sword and buildings razed. Even the king's own son, Lazlo, the governor of the town, was captured and hung in a crow cage to starve. The Wiccan have moved east to continue their trail of destruction, but the Wolfpaw clan have elected to stay behind in Carvel and make it a new home for their people. For now, outsiders are keeping a wide berth from the area and the town's refugees have since found solace in the southern towns of Fallow Heart and Moonwick.

Durnhollow: Following many decades of civil war and strife, the royalty of Valeron were keen to strengthen their position and that of the Church. Following the fervent witch hunts of his predecessor's reign, King Bevan gave authority to the newly appointed Lord and Lady Justice to better administer law and faith to the kingdom. As part of this initiative, they set up the inquisition dungeons at Durnhollow, choosing the remote location to ensure it was free of the corruption of the cities and to deter would-be prison breakers. Set within the remains of a dwarven mountain stronghold, this formidable prison is feared by all, for it is said that those that enter never leave – and many dark tales have been told of the methods employed by the inquisition to extract the truth from its prisoners.

Stone Ford: Situated at a key crossing point of the Vacherie Delta, Stone Ford had originally been seen as a frontier town, originally marking the western reach of Valeron influence in the days before Allam's crusade. Word had reached Stone Ford of the fall of Carvel and messengers were quickly dispatched to the capital requesting urgent aid. Unfortunately, the Wiccan army were swift in their advance and the town was sacked and put to the torch before aid could arrive. Driven by their vengeful fervour, the Wiccan did not tarry to gloat over their victory and have

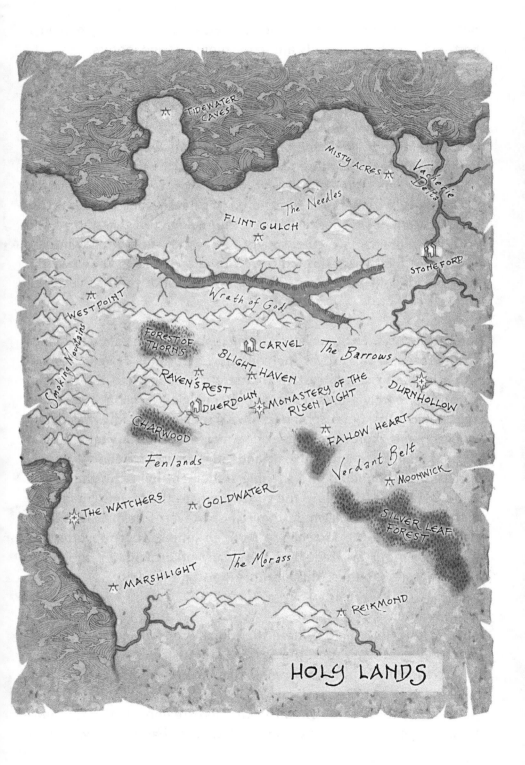

HOLY LANDS

continued marching onwards into the Heartlands, leaving behind a shattered ruin that is already attracting monsters and looters.

The Watchers: Nine immense stone guardians stand motionless along the rugged cliffs of the western coastline, staring out across the Mirrored Sea. No one knows who crafted these statues or whether they once had some form of life. Some believe they may have once been titans, the mythical creatures that taught the dwarves the ways of magic and runelore. Others speak of a legend of a mad wizard who crafted the statues himself to mark the direction of his final resting place – across the sea. Many have tried to fathom the meaning of the statues and some sea captains have even sought to navigate a path following the direction of their gaze. This led them to the archipelago known as the Coral Islands, but no mysterious treasure or burial site has yet been found.

Tidewater Caves: Erosion caused by the battering tides and chill winds of the Frozen Sea has, over the course of thousands of years, carved out an immense cavern system that stretches deep into the coast of the northern Holy Lands. Pirates and smugglers originally used the caves as hideouts, but it soon became a popular haven for whalers and explorers – even some Skards seeking a more forgiving habitat than that afforded them by their own bleak lands. This diverse meeting of people has led to the founding of a sizeable settlement built into the cavern network. Tunnels lead up to the surface, where the town's inhabitants can hunt, forage, and farm. In the vast sea caverns below, ships lie at anchor alongside the ramshackle wooden jetties where taverns and inns boast a profitable trade from the steady influx of pirates, smugglers and adventurers that use this location as a stop-off point.

Saskat Prairies

South of the Holy Lands, where the marshy fens give way to barren plains and weathered rock, the Saskat Prairies stretch for hundreds of miles, presenting a savage wilderness that Valeron has loosely laid claim to but failed to conquer.

The hostile nature of this untamed region, with its many predators and maze-like canyons and valleys, has kept invaders at bay and thwarted all but the most stalwart of explorers and hunters. Nevertheless, the prairies have many valuable resources, from the hides and ivory of the bisons and mastodons, to the rare orchids and dahlia that grow within the deep valleys – desired by alchemists for their potent properties. It is also rumoured that vast caverns within the mountains and crags are riddled with deposits of gold and silver, and even dwarven treasures.

The Halli are the most prolific of the human populations found in the prairie lands. Believed to have a common ancestry with the Wiccan, the Halli are a nomadic people, who typically follow the paths of the migrating herds as they range across the prairies. Whilst some outsiders may label them as primitive savages, the Halli have a deep and rich culture, and their skilled horsemanship coupled with their intimate knowledge of the landscape, has garnered them a grudging respect by both friend and foe.

Nawa: The Halli wander the plains and valleys, never settling for more than a few days in any one area. However, once every year all the tribes converge beneath the shadows of the mountains to bury the bones of their dead, and to pay their respects to their ancestors. This site, known as Nawa (which means 'gift' in the Halli language) serves as their only permanent settlement, a walled town built on the banks of a mountain river. One tribe is chosen every five years to settle in Nawa and act as its protective guardians. It is a position of great honour amongst the tribes to protect their sacred lands and should any ill befall the town, then its guardians would be outcast from Halli society. The town itself has two districts – with non-Halli visitors and settlers confined to the outer section, whilst the inner section of the town is for Halli only.

Nautica: Situated on the westernmost peninsula of the prairie-lands, the port of Nautica started life as a research camp founded by the Alchemical and Botany Society. Originally set up to study the marine wildlife and local flora and fauna, the settlement soon became a stop-off point for merchant vessels travelling between Shale and the southern seas. Now a thriving port and operating beyond the prying eyes of Valeron authorities and the Church's inquisition, Nautica has become a

BUZZARD'S REST

RED ROCK MOUNTAINS

FARWATERS

DAZZLESCAR PEAKS

BLOODIED VALLEY

Goldgrass
Prairies

Twisted Canyons

SPIRIT POOLS

BRAMBLE DOWNS

Gnoll Hills

NAWA

TORKA'S FALL

GRESANOOK

SINGING WATERS

Kinuka Wilds

WINDSHEAR GULCH

Forlorn
Crags

Pride Lands

The Thorns

CAMP
HARRISON

NAUTICA

HOWLING
JUNGLE

MER-ROCK

Palm
Coast

SASKAT PRAIRIES

primary hub of magical learning and experimentation, and many of the Society's labs and vaults are now located within Nautica. The settlement also has trade with the reclusive Mer-folk and many of their number now live openly amongst the people – and often find work as crew as their seamanship abilities are highly-prized by captains.

Torka's Fall: These broken rock formations are believed to be the remains of a gigantic stone guardian that once protected the land and its people. The legends tell of a titanic battle between the guardian and a mated pair of elder dragons, who felled the giant with ice and fire, shattering its immense body into the fragmented ruin that can be seen today. The Halli still believe that there are magical enchantments woven into the ancient rock, which bestow protection and blessings on those who camp within their boundaries. Therefore, Halli tribes often use this location as a temporary base – and Valeron merchants have set up a small settlement here to trade with the Halli and provision them with Valeron steel and other luxury goods from the far reaches of the kingdom.

Gresanook: In the western foothills, a gnoll fort clings to the sides of a rocky wind-blasted crag. Little more than a series of huts, caves and rickety walkways, this settlement serves as a base for the gnolls to launch raids against merchant caravans and Halli camps, and mount scavenging expeditions into the river valleys and canyons. The gnolls share a common ancestry with their goblin cousins, but have evolved into a hardier stock, better able to suit the demanding environment in which they live. Whilst most of their number possess only a rudimentary intelligence, they do display a keen instinct for pack tactics, which can make them formidable opponents when numbers are on their side. The current leader of Gresanook is believed to be a gnoll wild mage of some talent, which suggests that a few of these savage beasts have the intellect to master the arcane arts and impose order over their rough and brutish brethren.

Camp Harrison: Beyond the Kinuka Wilds, where prides of black lions stalk their prey, and harpies roost amongst the crags and twisting river canyons, there is a walled camp that serves as a supply post for those seeking to explore the wilds or strike out south into the steamy northern reaches of the Terral Jungle. Founded by renowned trophy hunter, Tomir Harrison, the settlement is now run by his great granddaughter, Reema Harrison. Fuelled by fierce ambition, Reema is now seeking to expand the camp into a thriving trade port, which might one day rival the pirate port of Sheril. Already, efforts have been made to set up jetties and warehouses along the coast, and trade agreements have been forged with pirate captains and privateers who ply the Cerulean Sea. These new allegiances have given the camp hunters greater access to distant markets, from the souks of Khitesh to the arcades of Venetia – all of whom will pay high prices for the exotic goods the hunters can provide, such as ivory, pelts, magical reagents, and even live animals from the jungle and prairie-lands.

The Terral Jungle (and Bone Basin)

Valeron loosely lays claim to the lush and teeming rainforest of the Terral Jungle, but none have been able to tame its wilds or even adequately map its interior. The landscape is an unforgiving gauntlet of tangled vines and roots, muddy swamps, impassable cliffs and churning rapids. And that's not even taking into account the deadly ecosystem where each and every living organism is in brutal competition for survival, with the apex predators, such as the giant carnosaurs and savage tigris, dominating all.

Within the steamy depths of the jungle, some of the oldest human ruins can be found – lost cities that trace their ancestry back to the ancient Lamuri, a people whose culture once flourished but was brought to a swift end by a demonic invasion and their own hubris. The ruins still speak of this once proud people, from the pillared courtyards and immense ziggurats, to grand halls and elaborate burial chambers. Most of these places are shunned by the indigenous tribes and hunters of the region, for some warped magic still clings to the crumbling stonework, giving life to malevolent spirits and corrupting the deadly predators that stalk in their shadows.

To the south, Dormus' distant past as a volatile molten world is still evident in its active chains of volcanoes and steaming rivers of magma. Past these charred and barren wastes, the rugged land gives way to a sunken basin that was once an ocean, before seismic turmoil cut it off from the surrounding seas. Broiling underground temperatures, as well as the many crevices and fissures that crisscross the area, may have been the cause for the gradual draining of seawater, leaving behind a dangerous desert of quicksand and chasms that make navigating this region a deadly endeavour.

Clearwater Cay: This bustling coastal town welcomes visitors from all parts of Dormus, whether they be pirates, smugglers, slavers or even Venetian princes. Situated on a rocky bluff that overlooks the tropical waters and sandy beaches of the coast, Clearwater Cay has a haphazard layout, built on many elevations as the land rises steeply, its cliffsides riddled with smugglers' tunnels and caves. Rowdy markets and taverns see men and women of all walks of life rubbing shoulders, sharing tales of the high seas, and doing business – some legitimate but most of it shady. A popular saying in town is, 'see but don't say in Clearwater Cay, else you'll be dancing in Betsy's bay' – a reference to the notorious pirate queen, whose phantom ship and undead crew are often sighted in the waters and sandy isles along the coast.

Jade Spires: Recent earthquakes have opened up a previously unreachable valley, nestled within a range of mountains. A panicked survivor of an ill-fated hunting trip spoke of a vast Lamuri city, choked by vines and creepers. Since then, explorers have bravely ventured into the valley and have reported on what they found. Unlike many of the other ruins found within the Terral Jungle, this city appears to have developed well beyond the period that the Lamuri civilization was assumed to have met its end. Even its architecture, which features grand towers rising up out of the encroaching undergrowth, hints at other influences at play in its development. This find, now known as the 'Jade Spires' is drawing explorers and adventurers in their droves – those willing to face the perilous dangers of this mysterious newfound city to uncover its treasures and secrets.

Tartarus: Built within the mouth of a once dormant volcano, this dwarven city has a storied history, being the final resting place of the demon sword known as Ragnarok. When the archdemon, Barahar, advanced south with his demonic army, it was the dwarves of Tartarus

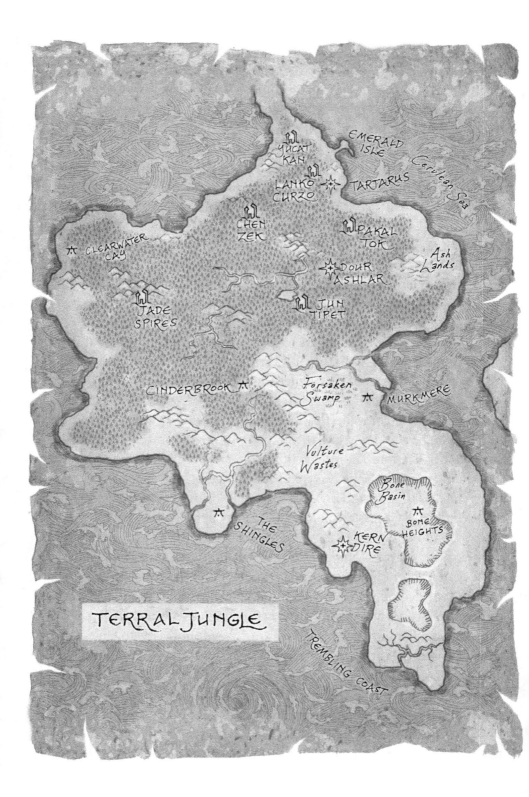

TERRAL JUNGLE

who mounted a spirited defence and defeated the archdemon by shattering his blade. In doing so, the trapped souls within the blade were unleashed on an already ravaged city. The beleaguered dwarves quickly set about destroying their portals to ensure the corruption could not spread to other cities. Isolated from their brethren, the dwarves fought hard to reclaim their city, but gradually fell to the taint that had been unleashed – a terrible and sentient evil that steadily transformed their once magnificent city into a nightmarish shadow of its former glory; one that held no escape for those trapped within.

Murkmere: The scalding rivers and maze-like mangroves of the Forsaken Swamp present a daunting challenge to those seeking to plunder the waters of their rare resources. Nevertheless, many have been willing to try and fortunes have been made by both the desperate and the foolhardy – all of which has led to a steady influx of travellers willing to test their mettle against this inhospitable region. To that end, the town of Murkmere has risen to become a surprising success story despite the hazards of its environment. Lurking as a series of bridges, walkways and repurposed fishing vessels, this sizeable settlement has earned the nickname 'ghost town' on account of its ramshackle buildings forming a shifting, indistinct outline amidst the persistent haze. Here, barges can be hired to travel out into the vast wetlands, with experienced guides and hunters at the helm, providing protection from the many dangers that lurk within the fetid waters.

Bone Heights: When the waters of the trapped ocean receded, what was left behind was a veritable treasure trove of wrecked ships, mysterious ruins and the skeletal remains of colossal sea beasts. It is the latter that has given the settlement of Bone Heights its name, set within the ribcage of a gargantuan creature that would have once hunted within the ocean depths. The town serves as a supply hub for the experienced hunters and adventurers who are willing to navigate the dangerous seabed, searching out its lost treasures and exploring the strange ruins that hint at some ancient race. Many secrets wait to be discovered for those brave enough to seek them, but the dangers are legion – from the chittering colonies of giant insects to the immense sand snakes that can blend invisibly against the glittering sands.

The Contested Lands

In ancient times, the Kingdom of Franklin once rivalled that of Valeron, and may well have succeeded it had it not been for the Mordland incursion that devastated the region. The Frankish towns and cities could not withstand the merciless barbaric hordes that poured in from the east. One by one they fell to ruin as Mordland pushed ever westwards in a bid to destroy all in its wake and add the territory to their already expansive empire. Eventually, Valeron came to the aid of its neighbour, and was able to bolster the defences of the last remaining Frankish city, Lull. The Mordlanders were defeated, but it was a pyrrhic victory for the Franks. Their land was now in ruin and thousands of lives had been lost. Ever the opportunist, Valeron claimed the war-torn lands as their own and Lull was absorbed into the kingdom – although, even to this day, those of Frankish decent have held a bitter enmity for their Valeron saviours, who they blame for not acting sooner to achieve a decisive victory and prevent the monumental losses of that bloody war.

The land was steadily resettled but would always remain a theatre of war. This was true even in Judah's day, when the One God's messiah ventured eastwards with his anointed apostles. Here he was to meet his end, but not before he founded the holy site of Antioch that would later expand into a devout city of pilgrims.

Countless centuries of war have left their mark on what is now known as the Contested Lands. What had once been a verdant wilderness is now a barren wasteland of scorched ruins, spirit-haunted forests and abandoned settlements left to decay. The many wars and its resulting anguish have torn much of the fabric of the physical realm, leaving it victim to the influence of the Norr. The shades of dead warriors and grave knights now roam the necropolises, while vile corruptions spread their rot and decay throughout the forests and valleys, leaving a tortured landscape in their wake.

Antioch: Although the holy city has fallen to ruin, Valeron is forever keen to reclaim it from the monsters and Mordland raiding parties that befoul its many shattered streets and dilapidated buildings. For the Church, Antioch once represented the might of the One God, symbolically represented by the glittering white citadel that stands at its center. Known as 'The Divine Vigil', this citadel was summoned into being by

CONTESTED LANDS

Judah when he planted his rod into the earth. No creature of evil intent can pass close to its walls, so it has always remained untouched by the ravages of war. Holy crusaders still seek to defend Antioch and restore the city to its past glory, but their numbers are few and the perils of the land many. Nevertheless, the Church has not lost hope in one day resettling Antioch and using it as a strategic base to launch further crusades eastwards.

Lull: The capital and last remaining city from the times of the Franks, Lull is a physical embodiment of the changing fortunes of a once proud people. The old paintings and tapestries depict a grand city of spires, stretching into bright azure skies – its avenues winding past statues of heroes and kings, its central castle adorned in colourful banners that celebrated the impressive majesty of its storied rulers. Today, Lull is a city of poverty and disease, its streets now infested with rats and thieves. The spires may still stand proud against melancholy skies, but their scorched and crumbling structures speak of misery and squalor. Beneath the city, a maze of fetid sewer tunnels leads into a vast cavern network known as 'The Under Court'. This subterranean expanse is rumoured to be a kingdom unto itself, ruled over by a clan of ratlings – and believed to be the source of the plagues that frequently sweep the city.

Halls of Light: On his journey eastwards, Judah and his apostles made a detour into the dwarven ruins known as Khar Dural. The mountain region had always been avoided by travellers, even foolhardy adventurers, as it was known to be haunted by the spirits of its fallen dwarven inhabitants. Judah had heard their anguished cries and sought to free them from their pained limbo. Wielding the holy light, Judah and his followers descended into the depths, battling the creatures that had made its halls their own, and releasing the spirits from their torment. One of Judah's disciples was a former bard who would later become famous for composing the ballad 'The Halls of Light', which would give the place its name. Pilgrims soon moved into the ruins in an effort to transform its expansive chambers into a holy site to venerate the One God. However, it was not long before the creatures of the underworld claimed it once again.

Faceless Court: The many kings of ancient Franklin each had their own legends, often involving the strange enchantress who would bless their weapons and armour before battle. The people looked up to their kings as fabled heroes, whose might on the battlefield was unsurpassed. To venerate such heroes, the slopes of the mountain range now known as the Horns of Khali, once had immense portraits of each noble king carved into their rock. Since those days, Mordland raiders have defaced the portraits, either hacking away features or carving their own mockeries atop that of the original Frankish sculptures. Hence, the grisly display is now known as the Faceless Court – a monument of woe, that presides over the battle-ravaged plains below.

Curse Wood: This blighted forest is characterized by its towering dark trees and malevolent spirits. Once, the forest had been a flourishing paradise, nurtured and protected by its elder tree and dryad guardians. Ever since war and strife came to the Contested Lands, and with it the plagues and corruption from the Norr, the forest has become a place of shadow. It is believed the dryads still dwell at its centre, but they are now warped by the dark energies of the Shroud and the elder tree they were sworn to protect is now a twisted and malformed creature, its roots sunk deep into the corrupted leylines that feed its malign existence.

The High Places: The Mordland people worship many demon patrons, who demand sacrifices and debased rituals as part of their worship. In return for such devotion, the demons gift their followers with nefarious magics and enchantments. The hills that overlook the Mordland city of Shinar serve as a grisly symbol of this unholy covenant. The flayed skins of their enemies cover the sides of wooden structures that reach high into the skies in mockery of the holy citadel that stands amidst the ruins of Antioch. Diabolic idols hang from human hair, twisting and rocking in the chill winds – and at night it is said that infernal lights dance about these ghastly trophies, beneath which the Mordlanders perform their dances and rituals, and burn offerings to please their demon masters.

The Badlands
South of the Perovan mountains, the land descends into vast grassland prairies and rugged swathes of pine forest, before meeting a dry

and near endless desert wasteland. Throughout the ages, this vast region has had little to offer its surrounding nations, from Khitesh and Valeron, to ancient Perova. It wasn't until the discovery of diamonds and gold in the early 1300s that a sudden influx of prospectors and miners flooded into the area, looking to make quick fortunes and tame this savage wilderness.

The gold rush era was short-lived and many settlements and towns quickly abandoned to be swallowed up by the dust and desert. However, the stories and songs of such times has created a romantic image of a life on the frontier, where the abundant land offers up fresh possibilities for settlement, and the deep forests and crags may still conceal hidden riches waiting to be uncovered.

Hence, the Badlands has continued to draw many south into the vast canyons and plains, lured by such dreams of starting a new life – and for some, a more ambitious goal of venturing across the harsh Cinder Lands into Khitesh, where exotic cities and paradise vistas are promised to those who are willing to run such a gauntlet.

Alas, such dreams are often shattered as people face the realities of life on the frontier – where towns draw outlaws and smugglers, and those simply down on their luck, and where violence and bloodshed are common place. Travel through the region is hard and perilous, not only due to the searing temperatures, but also the myriad of dangerous predators that prey on the unwary – from packs of wild dogs and wolves to sand spiders and wyverns.

Crown Mesa: Some may hold up the existence of Crown Mesa as a triumph of human ingenuity and resourcefulness, others may simply see it as an example of the worst of humanity. Set atop a giant rock, the main town is a sprawling heap of shacks, many built one on top of another forming precarious structures. Beneath this ramshackle eyesore, the steep walls of the rock itself are riddled with tunnels and walkways, hinting at the vast caverns within where people live and trade. Out on the plains, the wretchedness of humanity continues to spill out in a maze of tents and rickety shacks, amidst piles of rubbish and refuse that form their own steaming landscape of squalor. Crown Mesa is very much a symbol of the broken dreams of those that came south looking for something better, but having being beaten by the

THE BADLANDS

cruel environment, have instead been drawn together for survival – forming their own frontier civilization out of the ashes of their many disappointments.

Tombstone: Tombstone was a mining town that sprang up at the height of the gold rush era, when gold and diamonds were discovered in the nearby crags and caverns. As with most of the region, such treasures were quickly plundered and further finds became less frequent. Many chose to simply move on, but some made the brave decision to stay and make a go of their new lives on the frontier. In recent years, there is talk of travellers going missing in the town – and stories that describe a dark and brooding place, its people dour and suspicious of outsiders. There is even rumour that the people have suffered a curse and are now stricken with lycanthropy, which may explain the strange chorus of bestial howls that are often heard in the region of the Grey Pines.

Arabah: Long before the gold rush era, a Khiteshi prince ventured north and founded the town of Arabah. Legends recount that he was led to the banks of the Spiderweb River by a genie, who promised him great riches should he build a great temple to venerate the demon lord, Azariah. The prince answered this call and set about creating a grand structure that was intended to reach the very heavens. Alas, some terrible catastrophe befell the people before the tower could be completed. Some accounts describe a plague, others speak of a rain of fire that destroyed the tower and demolished the settlement – all at the behest of a rival demon who was angry at Azariah's arrogance. In the end, the town was left as a ruin, but the stories have not deterred explorers and adventurers travelling to this remote location, in an effort to hunt out the prince's treasures and retrieve his powerful genie.

Huron Gates: Anyone intending to make the journey by land into northern Khitesh must pass through the mountain fortress known as the Huron Gates. Named after a hero of Khiteshi legend, this impressive structure spans a narrow pass, which serves as both a border garrison and supply camp. Guides and caravans can be hired from the Huron Gates to take travellers south across the desert, to either the coastal capital of See-Val or the town of Sand Port. For many centuries, the fortress has been largely under-manned and left to ruin as Khitesh no longer sees the protection of its northern borders a concern, and fewer travellers are choosing to make the dangerous overland crossing into Khitesh.

Acknowledgements

A huge thank you to all those who backed the Kickstarter and helped to make this book a reality. And a special shout out to those legendary heroes who went the extra mile to prove their valour and loyalty. May your loot always be epic!

Hall of Heroes
Anatrok, Hamad Alnajjar, Darren Arquette, Stefan Atanasov, Rene Batsford, Shaun Bennett, Ian Berger, Eddie Boshell, Andy Bow, Brett Bozeman, Bruce Brown, Greg Burgess, Nicholas Chin, James Cleverley, Michael Cohen, Cristina Conforti, Rob Crewe, Adolfo De Unánue, Steven Dean, Pete Flynn, Calvin Freemore, Jamie Fry, Marco Gariboldi, Fabrice Gatille, Tom Geraghty, David Gotteri, John Marc Green, Ian Greenfield, Stephen Griffin, Heiloku, Kay Hiatt, Robin Horton, Adrian Jankowiak, Christopher Jappy, Magnus Johansson, Mark Lain, Steven Langer, Ben LaRose, Y. K. Lee, Michael Lee, Stuart Lloyd, Gordon 'Draco Wolfsbane' MacLeod, Adam Mann, Harrington Martin, Martin Metzler, Tim Meyers, Greg Muri, Ang Nam Leng, Mary O'Malley, Ant O'Reilly, Oliver Peltier, Rich E Petch, Charles J. Revello, Wendy Shakespeare, Andrew Paul Sheerin, Kashif Sheikh, Luke Sheridan, Matt Sheriff, John Simpson, R. Smith, Simon Smith, Jason South, Richie Stevens, Geoff Thirlwell, Joe Tilbrook, Steve Truong, Renato Tuason, VidjaGamez, Kevin Wales, Todd Weigel, Fengal Wildmane, Andrew Wright, Ian Yeo, Benjamin Soh Beng Yong.

Avatars of Light
Teofilo Hurtado, Kurono, David Poppel, Ralf Steinberg, Adriano Ziffer.